## 'No need to rus~~h~~ ~~...~~
## all night.'

All night. With Cade. ~~...~~ ~~...~~ ~~...desire~~ she saw in the depths of his eyes, the strength she felt in his arms. Why did Belle feel as if she'd just jumped off a cliff? And why wasn't she scared?

Oh, but she was scared. And excited.

And the combination was more tantalizing than she'd ever thought possible. In the arms of a man she had just married, yet barely knew, a wildness swept through her. A rush of yearning so strong it took her breath away.

Cade trailed a hand over her bare shoulder, then ran his fingertips along her lacy neckline. 'I like your dress.'

'Dress?' She blinked. 'Oh, yes. Thanks, I, uh, bought it in Italy.' Belle struggled to concentrate as Cade continued his sensual exploration.

'You look great in it.' He nuzzled his way to her ear. 'But I'm going crazy thinking about what you'll look like out of it...'

Dear Reader,

As an avid movie fan with a fondness for films of the thirties and forties, I've always loved the stylish *It Happened One Night*. A flash of Claudette Colbert's shapely leg gave hitchhiking a whole new dimension, and the sight of Clark Gable's bare chest sent undershirt sales plummeting. Now, I don't expect my hero, Cade McBride, to set any national trends, but I hope he'll make a few readers' hearts beat faster. He's a bit of a rogue, and definitely not the marrying kind, but when Belle Farentino has to have a husband, Cade's her man. In more ways than one.

Although their 'marriage' gets off to a rocky start, these two soon discover that love doesn't always play by the rules...but the heart always plays for keeps.

Happy reading,

Sandy Steen

P.S. I love to hear from my readers!

# AFTER THE LOVING

## BY
## SANDY STEEN

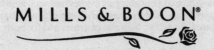

MILLS & BOON®

*MILLS & BOON and MILLS & BOON with the Rose Device
are registered trademarks of the publisher.
TEMPTATION is a registered trademark of
Harlequin Enterprises Limited, used under licence.*

*First published in Great Britain 1998
by Harlequin Mills & Boon Limited,
Eton House, 18-24 Paradise Road, Richmond, Surrey TW9 1SR*

© Sandy Steen 1997

For Harry,
Because he always makes me laugh.
And because his heart holds so much love.

My thanks and appreciation to Jenny Hyatt, a terrific aunt, who
might have missed her calling as the best research assistant on
planet Earth. And to Dana Bindeman of Pine Ridge
Quarterhorses, for all her help and patience, and for being family.

ISBN 0 263 80811 4
21-9803

*Printed and bound in Great Britain
by Caledonian International Book Manufacturing Ltd, Glasgow*

# 1

FROM THE BAY WINDOW of the Farentino study, Cade watched the Suburban come to a halt in front of the house. The door opened, and for several seconds Belle struggled with a reluctant seat belt before swinging her long legs out of the truck. Lord, but that skirt was short, he thought, reminding himself not to drool. Never mind that it was Italian silk with a matching jacket. If that was her idea of proper attire, he was definitely in the wrong business. She walked toward the house, then stopped and went over to the fountain in the middle of the courtyard. She sat down, crossed those gorgeous legs of hers and stared straight ahead.

Cade knew she had been to the lawyer's office for the reading of her grandfather's will. He also knew he should be ashamed of his lustful thoughts, considering Caesar had been gone less than two weeks. But he defied any man to look at Isabella Farentino and not want her. She was tall and slender with full breasts, and had the kind of mouth that could spice up a man's fantasies for years. She was graceful and intelligent. Most of all, she was the sexiest woman Cade had ever laid eyes on, and he had eyed more than his fair share.

The old man might not have been shocked at his appraisal, but he sure as hell would have been shocked to learn the dusty cowboy he had hired three years ago to ramrod the twelve-hundred-acre Farentino working ranch did more than simply admire his beautiful granddaughter. Cade doubted Caesar would appreciate knowing his foreman lay awake nights thinking about her, only to fall asleep dreaming about her.

Not that it could ever be anything but a dream. Women like Belle didn't belong with a man like him. Cade's family might have lived in Sweetwater Springs for three generations, but his ancestors were horse thieves, alcoholics and plain old cowboys. Belle had never known anything but wealth and security born of tradition, knowing she had a place in a loving family. Except for his time on the rodeo circuit, he had spent his adulthood rambling until Caesar gave him a chance at something better. She was silk and soft fragrances. He was leather and the smell of horses.

The two didn't mix.

He had forgotten that once, and he had paid for it with self-loathing. The only trouble was he couldn't forget. Even now, Cade could recall his encounter with Belle as if it had happened an hour ago.

He'd been foreman barely three months when Belle

returned from Europe, and the first time he saw her, he knew she was trouble. Because he wanted her. She radiated sensuality the way the sun radiates heat. But it wasn't overt or fake. That's what made her so hard to resist. If she had come on to him, he could have dismissed her without a backward glance. But she hadn't. He told himself she wasn't his kind of woman. She was too young, and far too well-bred. The bottom line was that she was out of his class and he knew it. What could a cowboy like him ever hope to offer a lady like her? Then one night after a ride, she came into the barn while he was mucking out stalls and forking hay. The instant he saw her, he should have set the pitchfork aside and walked out. Instead, he'd stayed and talked. And wanted. He could still remember how good she smelled, wearing a light floral scent that made him think of fields of bluebonnets. It wasn't much of a stretch to think of the two of them, together, in those fields. She'd looked downright delicious in a pair of jeans that fit her sweet little fanny the way his hands itched to, and a cream-colored silk blouse that set off her tan. Thank God she had declined his offer to help her unsaddle her horse, because within five minutes he was so hard he could barely move.

But he was a sucker for punishment.

Leaning a gloved hand on his pitchfork, he had watched her groom the filly, watched her bottom wiggle as she brushed, watched her breasts strain against the silk as she stretched and reached. Meanwhile, every good reason he had given himself to stay away from her disappeared like the first raindrops ending a drought. He didn't remember actually walking over to her, but if he lived to be a hundred he would never forget the way she looked at him when he called her name. She turned, her eyes so soft and compelling a man could forget his own name, much less self-denial. And before he knew it, he was kissing her.

Need obliterated good sense. He didn't even bother to remove his work gloves before hungrily pressing her body to his. Only when they came up for air and he saw his dirty glove prints on her silk blouse did reality smack him in the face. If he had been a churchgoing man, he might have thought it was a sign from the Almighty. But Cade didn't need God to tell him to take his filthy hands off her. He knew he didn't deserve something as fine and rare as Belle. He was so angry at himself, he practically shoved her away, telling her she was a little too inexperienced for his tastes. Cruel words, he knew, but they had done the trick. And even if he regretted them, he told himself it was for her own good. He'd been telling himself that ever since.

No, despite the fact he and Caesar had forged a friendship based on respect and trust, Cade knew he was not the kind of man the aging vintner had pictured with his only granddaughter. That knowledge had been Cade's insurance policy, making it easy for him to stay away from Belle. But now she was in charge and he would have to work directly with her. No buffer. No acceptable excuse for avoiding her. And he wasn't sure he could do it.

Ironically, if Caesar had lived, Cade would be making plans to leave now instead of wondering if he still had a job. They had made a handshake agreement, only a few days before the old man's heart gave out, that would have set Cade up with his own land. His own place. But now, well, he would have to keep working, saving.

So, he'd come today to see if he still had a free hand running the ranch, and to see if Belle might be considering moving into town. The ranch was a good two miles from Sweetwater Springs and the winery office. Being so far out had its disadvantages, particularly now that she was alone. Of course, Posey, the housekeeper, was around, and as manager of the winery, his friend, Reese Barrett, was usually nearby, but they weren't family.

The truth, when Cade felt up to facing it, was that he didn't like the thought of Belle being alone. Worse, he didn't like the fact that there was nothing he could do about it.

Still watching her, Cade frowned. She wasn't coming inside. Maybe the reading of the will had been harder on her than he'd expected. As if to confirm his observation, she leaned forward and put her head in her hands. Cade's heart lurched. Was she crying? Oh, God, don't let her be crying. Should he go to her? Maybe she didn't want him, or anyone, to see her crying.

But he wanted to go to her. So bad, the need was a like a dull ache around his heart. To be honest, he hadn't come today just to check on his job. He'd wanted to see how she was coping with Caesar's death. To see if there was anything she needed, anything he could do for her. Even though he knew her pride might prevent her from asking or accepting anything he offered, he still had to come. But watching her now, he couldn't decipher her mood. Maybe, he decided, she just needed a moment to pull herself together.

Out in the courtyard, the more Belle tried to calm down, the angrier she got. The scene in Joseph Worthington's office played through her mind, over and over again. She still couldn't believe what her grandfather had done.

"That's barbaric!" she had insisted. "A—a throwback to the Middle Ages."

"Well, under the circumstances, you've got every right to be upset, however—"

"Upset? Oh, I'm way past upset, Mr. Worthington."

Belle couldn't believe her grandfather was actually trying to maintain control of the business *and* her life

even after his death. He always thought he knew
what was best for her, whether she agreed or not.

"My grandfather has gone to great lengths to take
charge of my life. Last year he even tried to arrange a
marriage between me and a young man from Italy.
But this is too much. Even for Caesar Farentino."

"Now, Isabella, he thought he was looking out for
your best interests. He really thought you needed a
man to help you run the business. You know that you
and the winery were the two things he loved most in
the world."

Oh, yes, she knew how her grandfather had felt
about the winery. They'd shared that passion, that
dream—for the Farentino label not only to stand for a
hallmark of excellence, but to also have a world-class
reputation. They'd been in total agreement in that respect. But that's where they parted company. Caesar
insisted the wines be made using the Old World
methods and traditions. Belle wanted to incorporate
the old with the new, using technology and marketing techniques. But her grandfather was adamant
that things be done his way. Now he was using her
love against her. He knew she would do anything to
have control of the winery. He knew making wine
was in her blood, in her heart.

"If it makes you feel any better, I tried to dissuade
him."

"Don't blame yourself, Mr. Worthington. Once my
grandfather made up his mind to do something, it

took an act of God or Congress to change it. Usually God.''

As she looked at the legal document that now defined her future, her initial shock dissolved into simmering anger.

''Let me just...'' She took a deep, calming breath. ''Let me see if I understand the terms of the will correctly. If I marry within thirty days from today, and stay married for twelve months, the winery, and everything with it, is mine. If I don't marry, or if I should get a divorce before the year is out, everything goes to my great-uncle Rafael and his four sons.''

Worthington sighed. ''True, unfortunately. Of course, in that event you would be provided for with a yearly sum.''

''What about contesting the will?''

''You could, of course, but I have to say that if you intend to use senility as a basis for the case, your chances are slim to none. Caesar had a reputation for his business acumen even at age seventy. In my opinion, it would be a waste of time, and money.''

He was probably right. Besides, she didn't have the time.

Her thirty-day ''clock'' was ticking.

''So, I'm damned if I do and damned if I don't.''

Frustrated, and hurt at her grandfather's lack of faith in her abilities, she saw no way out of her dilemma.

''I'm afraid so, my dear. And as unfair as it sounds,

if you want the winery, then by hook or by crook, you've got to find yourself a husband."

Now, sitting in the sunshine, Belle closed her eyes and rubbed her right temple. She could still see the pity in Joseph Worthington's eyes. She was trapped and they both knew it. And he was right. She needed a husband.

*By hook or by crook.*

Or maybe both?

Worthington's words invoked an idea that rose from her chaotic thoughts like a phoenix rising from the ashes of her destroyed dream. It wasn't original, but it could work.

She didn't want to get married, but she needed a husband. So why couldn't she buy one? People had done it for centuries in Europe and Asia, and the practice still continued today. It was called making a good marriage. Her own great-grandparents had started out in just such a way. He'd been a gifted vintner with very little land, and she'd been the only daughter of a wealthy landowner. Maybe they didn't think of it as buying a spouse, but that's what it boiled down to.

How ironic, she thought, to be using her grandfather's own tactics to achieve her goals while sidestepping his. But could *she* go through with a marriage of convenience?

The more Belle thought about it, the more she decided the idea had merit. She had a talent for prob-

lem-solving that went hand in hand with her singular
determination to swing into action once the solution
was at hand. A talent that had served her far better
than her other legacy from her fiery Italian ancestry.
That emotional, passionate side of her nature never
failed to cause problems. It exposed her vulnerability
and diminished her control.

Just another one of the many things she and her
grandfather had disagreed about. He never hesitated
to display his passion. For his wife when she was
alive. For the vineyard. For life. And on more than
one occasion he had chided Belle for being so re-
strained. How often had he told her that she couldn't
fight her own nature? That someday she would know
that true passion was a thing to be celebrated, not
controlled or feared.

But passion had killed her parents. They had been
fearless, reckless and wildly in love. At the tender age
of twelve, Belle thought they were the most romantic
couple on earth, until the day they died in an auto ac-
cident. The police officer who had brought the news
stated that their car was going more than ninety miles
per hour when it collided with a moving van. Reckless passion had left her an orphan.

Now everyone she loved—her parents and grandparents—were gone. Love, like passion, was unde-
pendable.

Well, she would take practicality over passion any
day. There were ways to ensure a husband couldn't

touch the Farentino wealth. Obviously, her grandfather hadn't thought about a prenuptial agreement. The problem was not how, but who.

Reese Barrett, rodeo cowboy turned winery manager, was the first name that came to Belle's mind. He was smart, hardworking, and he knew enough about the business to be an asset. And, as a bonus, she really liked him. But after a few minutes' thought, Belle doubted Reese would go for it. He was definitely the most honorable man she had ever known. He would never marry anyone he didn't love. Besides, he was too much like her grandfather, too old-fashioned, too serious. And like Caesar, he thought the old ways were the best when it came to wine making. If these obstacles weren't enough, Belle always sensed a sadness about him.

Maybe she was being overly dramatic, but she thought the sadness hinted at pain in his past, possibly a lost love. Reese was a complicated man, appearing to go along with everybody while those sharp blue eyes of his never missed a thing. He was no pushover to be led around by a ring in his nose, either. And if the tales of his high school days were to be believed, he had done more than his fair share of hell-raising. In fact, Reese and his buddies, Logan Walker, Sloane Gates and Cade McBride, had a reputation for fast moves on and off the football field. Known as the Fearsome Foursome, they had been en-

vied as hometown heroes and emulated as the ultimate hell-raisers.

No, the more she thought about it, the more she
decided Reese wasn't a good candidate for her convenient marriage proposal.

There were several other names that came to mind,
but she quickly discarded each of them for one reason
or another. The fact was, most of the truly good men
in Sweetwater Springs were already married, and the
rest were too young, too old or worthless drifters and
cowboys.

Like Cade McBride.

As soon as the name popped into her head, Belle
dismissed it. Vehemently.

Oh, no, not Cade McBride. No way. He was dan-
gerous where women were concerned. Where she
was concerned. Been there, done that, she thought.
And learned a hard lesson.

Cade was definitely not in the running for her rent-
a-husband plan. Only one thing interested him—a
good time and a good-time woman. And she didn't
meet the criteria. He had made that painfully clear
three years ago.

Gnawing her bottom lip, she looked over at his
truck, thinking of the time she had personally experienced his admittedly devastating charm. Upon her
return home after a year in Italy, where she'd steeped
herself in the customs and traditions of wine making,
she had taken one look at Cade and fallen hard. She

knew he had a reputation with women, but she had made the near fatal mistake of letting her passion overrule her good sense. Yet even now, after all the pain, the memory of their one and only kiss clung to her like Napoleon brandy clinging to the inside of a fine crystal snifter.

One spring evening after a sunset ride, she had walked her horse into the barn and found Cade forking hay. He was shirtless, sweaty and breathtaking. She'd had to force herself not to stare as he worked, his body so powerful, so beautiful, he could have posed for Michelangelo's David.

Their meeting was accidental, but watching him, Belle realized that sooner or later she would have found a reason to be alone with him. She had wanted this from the moment they'd met, but hadn't the courage to do anything about it. Fate, it seemed, had taken a hand, and she was glad. Thinking back, she couldn't remember how it happened, but before she knew it, she was in his arms. She could still remember the feel of his mouth on hers, hot and demanding, the press of his body against hers, hard and eager. He'd kissed her as if he wanted to devour her. And she wanted to be devoured.

Belle shook her head as if to clear the image of the two of them locked in a heated embrace. That blaze of passion was short-lived and bought with precious dignity. In a matter of seconds she had gone from hunger to humiliation as he pushed her away, telling her he wasn't interested. After that stinging rejection, she'd been lucky to get out of the barn with an ounce of pride left. Cade McBride was the last man she would consider for marriage, no matter how convenient.

To be fair, he was the best foreman they'd ever had, almost doubling the ranching profits over the past three years. But that didn't alter the fact that he was what her grandmother would have called a "cad." He was also too much of a maverick to ever agree to her scheme, too interested in calling the shots and...

What was she doing even *thinking* about Cade? It wouldn't work. And even if it was remotely possible, she couldn't think of a reason compelling enough for him to entertain such a bizarre proposal. He drew a good salary, but he obviously wasn't interested in money or what it could buy him, because he certainly wasn't into fashion, and had owned the same truck for as long as she had known him. What drives a man like Cade? she wondered. Other than testosterone.

"Reality check, Belle," she whispered, standing. "You're not getting anywhere with this. Try to keep your thoughts organized...."

Suddenly, she remembered going through Caesar's desk shortly after the funeral in search of the scheduling pad he used to keep track of everything about the dual operations of the place—from planting and harvesting to breeding and branding. In it she had stumbled across a brief and curious entry:

*Agreed to co-sign for Cade. Six hundred acres. Hate to lose him. But looks like a good investment.* The entry was dated two days before her grandfather's death. The only possible interpretation was that Cade had come to Caesar for a loan to buy land. Was it possible he wanted a place of his own? If so, how bad did he want it? What would he be willing to sacrifice?

As soon as the question formed in Belle's mind, she knew it was born out of a thirst for revenge. She wasn't proud of it, but it was only human for her to want to get a little of her own back. That night in the barn, Cade had delivered a blow to her confidence that she'd managed to hide but never fully recovered from. As much as she hated to admit it, the thought of dangling something he wanted badly in front of him like a golden carrot had appeal. And she *had* inherited eight hundred acres in the hill country upon her mother's death. The idea would have been tempting for any man.

Belle sighed. Who was she kidding? She'd been asking herself what would make Cade willing to sacrifice a year of his life, when the real question should be, Was she willing to set aside her pride in order to have what she wanted? Her list of eligible grooms was short to nonexistent, and asking Cade to be her husband in exchange for land was no more insane than the idea itself. So he had broken her heart. Was she going to let her dream die because of him, too?

Granted, under normal circumstances, he was the

last man on earth she would marry, but the circumstances weren't normal. And the clock was ticking.

What choice did she have?

She would just have to make this work, she thought, walking toward the house. As long as she stayed in control, everything would be fine. As long as she protected her heart. She straightened her shoulders, steeling herself for what she had to do. If he turned her down, which was likely, she would survive. A little bruised, but she'd live.

Cade was in the study sitting in the tasting chair with his feet propped on the desk.

"Get your feet off the furniture," she ordered, taking the chair behind the desk.

"Hello, darlin'."

Cade McBride called women "darlin'" as if he had the right to. All women. For some reason Belle didn't care to examine too closely, the thought of being lumped in with all his buckle bunnies rankled. In fact, it grated on her nerves like fingernails across a chalkboard.

She glared at his boots. Slowly, as if he had nothing better to do for the next decade, Cade put his feet on the floor.

She looked tired, he thought. Those dark circles under her eyes had been there since the funeral, but she was still the most beautiful woman he had ever seen. Naturally sexy, she didn't even know her own power where men were concerned. He wasn't so hung up on himself that he couldn't admit Belle was an itch he'd never been able to scratch, but he had worked hard at ignoring it. After the one kiss they had shared, he had declared her off-limits. For all her coolness, that night he had seen a latent passion in her that scared the hell out of him. Mostly because her passion ignited his to the point that he forgot she was beyond his reach.

"So, how ya doing?"

"Fine," she snapped. Then she reminded herself a sharp response was not the best preamble to approaching him with her unorthodox proposal. "And…thank you for coming to the funeral," she added gently.

"Caesar was a good man. I admired him."

"He thought a lot of you, too."

More than once she had seen the two of them with their heads together over something concerning the ranch and had been amazed that two men from such different backgrounds enjoyed each other's company so much.

Cade took a deep breath and sat forward in his chair. "Thought I'd come by and see if you were planning any changes."

"In the ranch operations?"

He nodded.

"You've done an excellent job as foreman. I see no reason why you shouldn't keep on doing an excellent job. Unless…"

"Unless?"

"You were thinking of leaving?"

"Not anytime soon, darlin'. Caesar paid me a good wage and let me run things my way. Short of having my own spread and a harem, that's about as good as it gets."

There it was, the perfect opening. All she had to do was take it. But suddenly her courage faded as she fought old hurts and wounded pride. "You're lucky." Angry at her own cowardice, she yanked open a drawer, searching for the scheduling pad.

"Somebody put a burr under your saddle?"

"What?" Carefully, she withdrew the pad from the drawer and placed it on the top of the desk.

"You came in here like you were loaded for bear. What's going on?"

"It's nothing." Belle reached out to touch the pad, but stopped. Then, slowly, she smoothed a hand over the worn leather cover. "I'll...I'll manage."

He shrugged, drawing her gaze to those ridiculously broad shoulders of his. "Never doubted it. You may look like one of those empty-headed Paris models, but you got steel in your backbone."

It wasn't exactly every woman's fantasy compliment, but then, what had she expected? "I'm glad someone thinks so." Carefully, she turned the pages. "Grandfather sure didn't."

"Belle."

His voice was so soft it startled her. She looked up and found him staring at her. "He was tough on you at times, but he loved you. And he was proud of you."

She glanced away, unable to bear the pain of hearing those words from Cade when she had longed to hear them from her grandfather. She had known he loved her, but proud?

"But he didn't trust me." Her eyes burned with unshed tears, but she would not allow herself the luxury of crying. Not in front of Cade.

"Where'd you get a half-baked idea like that?"

Belle squared her shoulders, sitting straighter in her chair. "Maybe from the fact that he let you run the ranch however you wanted, but he saw little value in any of my ideas, no matter how efficient or effective they were. Maybe from the fact that he didn't even think enough of my abilities to leave me the one thing he knew I loved. The winery."

Cade had assumed she would inherit everything. She had worked alongside Caesar for the past two years, absorbing his expertise like a sponge. She was quick and smart, but more than that, he knew she had a real vision for making the winery a world-class name. Granted, the old man had resisted her efforts to wed wine-making traditions with modern marketing techniques, but she had never backed down. And she'd been right. Cade didn't know much about making wine, but he knew sound thinking when he heard it. And through Reese, he had heard enough to know

Belle had a genuine talent for making wine, and a savvy business sense.

"You telling me the old man didn't leave you the winery?"

"In a backhanded sort of way."

"Care to translate?"

"I can have it all, provided I find a man and hang on to him for a year."

"You're not making any sense."

Belle rose, walked around to the front of the desk and perched herself on the corner. When she crossed those long legs of hers, Cade had to remind himself not to stare. "Grandfather's will stipulates that I get everything if I marry within thirty days and stay married for a year."

"That's loco."

"You'll get no argument from me."

"And if you don't marry?"

"My uncle Rafael and his sons wind up with Farentino Winery, lock, stock and one-hundred-year-old aging barrels." At his frown, she added, "Don't worry. They won't be interested in running the ranch any more than grandfather was."

Cade unfolded his long, muscular frame from the chair and stood up. "Caesar was wrong to do that. He had no right to try to control you, then or now. You've worked hard, and you deserve the chance to show the world what you've got. Everybody's got a right to their dream."

The sympathy was unexpected. "Thanks, I...I'm sorry I snapped at you."

"I'll live."

They both fell silent. She was going to blow her chance if she didn't speak up soon. The only chance she might ever have. Belle swallowed, or at least tried to swallow the lump of fear in her throat. "Have...have you got a dream, Cade?"

"Oh—" one corner of his mouth lifted in a smile "—I guess that spread and harem would just about cover it."

"Seriously?"

He looked at her long and hard before answering. "Is that so surprising?"

"You wanting a place of your own, yes. The harem, no."

He laughed. "I figure once I've got the spread, the harem will just naturally follow."

She didn't doubt it. "Naturally."

"Something on your mind, darlin'?"

"I, uh, found a note in Caesar's scheduling pad about you and six hundred acres—"

"Yeah, we talked about him co-signing a note so I could get my own place, but now that he's gone... Well, guess it'll have to wait."

One roll of the dice, Belle thought, knowing it was the biggest gamble of her life. Just say it. "Maybe not."

"What?"

"How bad do you want your own land, Cade? I mean, would you be willing to—"

"Now, wait just a minute, Belle." He saw where she was heading and intended to cut her off at the pass. "You're not seriously considering what I think you're considering."

"Yes." She took a deep breath. "Cade—"

"Hold on—"

"Will you marry me?" Before he could answer, she added, "Think about it. There's a piece of land close to Austin that belonged to my mother and came to me when she died. Eight hundred acres. No one has touched it in over ten years, but I'm told it's choice property. It's yours. Of course, you could continue on as foreman for as long as you want to. All you have to do is—"

"Marry you."

She nodded, scared he would either walk away, laugh at her or haul her off to a padded cell. From the way he was staring at her, the padded cell was the front-runner. "I don't want you to jump to the wrong conclusion. This is strictly business. We would be legally married, but we wouldn't actually live together, and there wouldn't be any...you know..."

"Sex."

"Yes."

"For a year."

"Oh," she said, realizing what she was asking. "I

guess that kind of restriction might be impossible for a man of your, well...appetites.''

''You might say that.''

''Then, I suppose if you were discreet.'' It killed her to grant such a concession, but she had no choice. ''You know, just not in Sweetwater Springs—''

''Let me get this straight. You're willing to indulge my—what did you call it?''

''Appetites.''

''Right. Just so long as I keep it quiet. And in exchange for staying married to you for a year, I walk away with eight hundred acres of hill country?''

''Exactly.''

''Now you're the one who's loco.''

''No, I'm desperate.''

''One leads to the other. What are you going to do if I say no?''

Belle's spirit sagged. She wouldn't cry. She wouldn't! ''Find someone else. If they don't want land, I'll offer cash.''

''Just like that?''

''Just like that.''

And she would, too. He'd seen that look in her eyes before. The day her grandfather told her it was unheard-of for a woman to become a vintner. Again, the day she returned from Italy after learning from the best. Determination and pride. Pure and simple. She was going to do this, and she'd keep looking until she found some poor slob as desperate for money or property as she was for the winery.

"So, I guess you're not interested—"

"I didn't say that."

"But—"

"Give me a minute."

"O-okay," she said, shocked that he hadn't given her a flat no. A tiny flame of hope sprang to life. "Could I...would you like some coffee?"

"Fine."

He could throttle her, he thought as she left the room. She was hell-bent on having the winery, and God only knew what kind of man she would find. Probably some saddle tramp, or worse, someone who would take her for every cent she owned. She had no idea of the potential dangers in this situation. For all her polish and sophistication, she was green as a gourd when it came to men. What if she got hold of some guy who decided not to respect their "no sex" agreement after they were married? Talk about being behind the eight ball. The jerk could pull a little sexual blackmail and there would be nothing she could do about it for a year. The thought of some son of a bitch making her life miserable made Cade's hands tighten into fists.

He blew out a breath and glanced down at his boots as if the solution to the dilemma was written across his toes. In a few short thoughts he had gone from thinking of her yet-to-be-determined husband as a guy, then a jerk and finally a son of a bitch. The truth was, he didn't like the idea of another man with Belle.

There, the admission hadn't killed him.

But neither did it do anything to solve his problem. Namely, that he didn't want anything to do with her scheme, but he couldn't stand the thought of someone else being a part of it. He reminded himself that the reasons for not pursuing his desire three years ago still held. They weren't compatible. She was silk and he was leather. If he agreed to this, heartache was as sure as sunrise and sunset. If he didn't...

Then, there was the land.

Damned if she wasn't handing him his lifelong dream on a silver platter. How was a man supposed to walk away from something like that? All the years he had saved and planned, always thinking that maybe someday... Now someday could be tomorrow. And for Belle, too. They both could have their dreams. All he had to do was say yes.

Belle came back into the office with two cups of hot coffee. She handed Cade the one without cream, then calmly walked to a wing-back settee opposite the tasting chair, sat down and crossed her long, elegant legs.

Damn, Cade thought, all that and a dream, too. No, not exactly *all*. As much as he might wish otherwise, Belle wasn't part of the deal, and even if she were...

But what if she were? What if he could have the dream he never expected to have? The real dream.

Belle.

"Are you thinking about accepting my proposal?" she asked.

"Maybe." And maybe he had a proposal of his own. However they had come to this moment, Cade knew he had one chance to be with Belle, and this was it. So, it might not be the real thing, maybe not even the right thing, but if he let this chance go by, he would regret it for the rest of his life. "Still sure this is what you want?"

Her heartbeat jumped into overdrive. "Absolutely."

He had a choice. Now or someday. Him or another man.

Cade made his decision. "All right, I'll marry you. On one condition."

He could see that Belle's hand shook so badly, she was forced to set the coffee cup on a nearby table. "Name it."

Praying she didn't know he was bluffing for all he was worth, Cade answered, "One night."

She blinked. "I don't understand."

"I want one night. Just you and me, naked and alone."

Belle shot up from the settee. "That's out of the question."

Cade shrugged and turned to leave, but his heart

was on the floor, battered and bruised. He'd started to bluff, and he had to see it through. "Suit yourself."

"Wait! Can't we...isn't there some other way?"

He turned back. "One night. I pick the place. No restrictions. No regrets when the sun comes up." *For either of us,* he thought. "Those are my terms."

He could almost see the wheels turning in her head as her mind grappled with this new development. Finally, she looked him straight in the eyes and took a deep breath.

"Deal." She offered him her trembling hand.

Cade took it and, in one quick motion, pulled her into his arms. "Don't you think we should seal it with a kiss?" he said, knowing at the moment a cocky attitude was his best ally. Besides, he didn't trust himself to play it straight.

She put her hand on his chest and stopped him just inches short of her lips. "Our deal was for one night. The sun is shining."

Cade grinned. "Have it your way, darlin'. One night. Unless you change your mind...later."

With a cocky grin still on his lips, he turned and left.

# 2

"MIGHTY FETCHING."

Belle whipped around at the sound of Reese's voice. "I—I was just checking my, uh, lipstick." She waved her hand in the direction of the huge oval mirror hanging behind her in the foyer.

"Like I said, mighty fetching."

She exhaled deeply as she smoothed a hand over the full skirt of her dress. "I'm so nervous I could scream."

"Brides are supposed to be nervous."

"This isn't exactly a traditional wedding, and I hardly feel like a real bride."

She wished Cade hadn't seen fit to reveal the true status of their pseudo-marriage to Reese. But what was done was done. After all, the two men had been friends all their lives, and if anyone could be trusted with the details of their "arrangement," it was Reese.

"Well, you look like a real bride. Except for one thing." From behind his back, he produced a small bouquet of sweetheart roses and baby's breath.

"They're from Cade. I'm just the deliveryman."

Surprised, but delighted, she took the flowers.

"That was very nice of him." The delicate fragrance of roses wafted around her, and for a moment she could almost imagine this was the wedding day she'd dreamed about. But only for a moment.

"Too bad Caesar isn't here to give you away."

"You're our only witness, and that suits me just fine. Besides," she said, once again grounded in reality, "I have no doubt grandfather is looking down on this whole debacle with a self-satisfied smile on his face."

"Probably."

For the first time, she noticed how handsome he looked in his tan western-cut suit, polished brown lizard boots and chocolate-colored Stetson. "Say, you look pretty sharp yourself."

He removed his hat and bowed from the waist. "Thank you, ma'am."

"Have you, uh, talked to Cade this morning?"

"Yeah, and he's tied in just about as many knots as you are."

"You think he's having second thoughts?"

"I think you're both out of your minds."

"But you don't think he'll back out."

"No. Which only proves my point. Besides, he's already signed what he called 'the pre-nup from hell.'"

"Reese, I know this marriage must look like the ultimate fiasco, but I had no other choice."

"You could have asked me."

"I—I don't know what to say." In truth, she was

stunned. He had never given her any indication that he was interested in anything other than being a friend.

"Day late and a dollar short," he said. "Story of my life."

"I just never... If it's any consolation, yours was the first name I thought of."

"Then why didn't—"

"Because I didn't believe you would marry someone you didn't love."

Reese looked at her for a long moment. "You're right, I wouldn't."

"And you don't love me." It fell somewhere between a question and a statement, but she knew the answer, anyway.

He smiled. "No, but I sure do like you a helluva lot."

Belle smiled back, feeling more at ease than she had all morning. "I like you, too, but I think we'd make much better friends than we would lovers."

"Guess we'll never know," he told her with a wink, just as the doorbell rang.

Belle almost jumped out of her skin, thinking Cade had arrived early. Instead, she was relieved to see Sam Overton, the justice of the peace. While Reese ushered Sam inside, Belle checked her hair and makeup in the mirror one more time.

Maybe she shouldn't have worn white. The lace-over-silk dress with its fitted bodice, cap sleeves and a full skirt was understated but definitely white as snow. What if Cade took one look at the dress and thought she was a virgin? Not that she had been promiscuous, but neither was she without experience. Not *that* much experience, but—

"Oh, stop it," she whispered.

Annoyed with herself, she touched the single strand of pearls around her neck. Her mother's pearls. Oh, no, she couldn't start getting sentimental over a make-believe wedding. Nothing about today was real except for the legalities.

And tonight.

Cade's only stipulation to their agreement. Tonight she would discover where their unfinished kiss would lead them. Tonight she would get the answer to the question she had asked herself after that kiss. What would it be like to be devoured by Cade Mc-Bride?

She shivered at the prospect. While a part of her wanted to run as far as she could, another part was almost...eager. Did that make her a fool or a wanton, after what had happened between them? Either way, anticipation jangled her nerves. If she was honest with herself, she had to admit part of her nervousness centered around what he would think of her as a lover. Three years ago she'd been a twenty-four-year-old love-struck young woman with stars in her eyes. Today, she was a little wiser. She knew how to protect her heart.

Still, it was natural for her to wonder how she'd rank in his long list of conquests. She'd only been with two men, and both had been gentle lovers. But she expected no tenderness from Cade. This was no well-bred house cat she was dealing with, but a tiger. Belle realized that pretend marriage or not, she wanted Cade to want her. Call it payback, or salving her wounded pride, but she wanted him to remember her, and their night together, for a long time. She hated the little barbs of self-doubt stabbing at her composure, but she couldn't seem to stop them. What if she wasn't any good? What if somehow she wasn't...enough?

The doorbell rang, and she jumped again. Reese brushed past her. "Easy does it."

He opened the door, and there stood Cade.

If Belle hadn't already been numb from nervous tension, her mouth would have fallen open in surprise. He looked—well...her mind scrambled over *handsome*, tripped over *gorgeous* and fell flat out in front of *breathtaking*. Absolutely breathtaking.

Her gaze started at his black snakeskin boots, traveled up the trim line of his black western-cut suit and crisp white shirt, to the bolo tie with an onyx stone set in silver. And the view just kept getting better, right up to the square line of his jaw and that smile that never failed to make her stomach do a little hop, skip and jump.

"Hello, darlin'."

"Hel..." She cleared her throat. "Hello, Cade."

Cade did some looking of his own, and what he saw made his head spin. She was stunning. Was it just the way the light was shining on her, or did she really look all soft, and sort of glowing? How could a wedding dress look elegant and sexy as hell at the same time? She was the most beautiful woman he'd ever seen, and she was all his, if only for one night.

Belle needed to take a deep breath, but she couldn't quite accomplish it with him staring at her like... Like he already knew how it would be with them tonight. Not just undressing her with his eyes, but visualizing them together, naked and needing.

"We were wondering if you'd hightailed it across the state line," Reese said.

Cade didn't take his eyes off Belle. "Would you if you had a woman who looked like that waiting for you?"

Without waiting for an answer, Cade stepped around him and offered Belle his arm. "You ready to get this show on the road, darlin'?"

Belle gazed up at him and fought a strangling panic rising like a tide. She could still back out. All she had to do was turn and... No. No, this was her idea. This was what she wanted.

She slipped her arm through Cade's. "Yes."

They walked into the parlor, where a smiling Sam Overton was waiting. "You folks ready to tie the knot?" he asked as they stood before him.

Cade put his hand over Belle's where it rested on his arm and leaned close to whisper, "Last chance to change your mind."

She glanced up at him. "And for you." He shook his head. "Me, neither," she whispered back.

"Go ahead," Cade told the J.P.

Overton cleared his throat. "We are gathered here today to unite this couple in the bonds of matrimony..."

Belle was glad they had chosen a justice of the peace instead of getting married in a church. Somehow this kind of ceremony made the marriage feel less real, less binding. She touched her mother's pearls again. But if that was true, then why did she suddenly feel as if her entire family was looking down from heaven wearing disapproving frowns?

"Do you, Ethan Cade McBride, take this woman..."

Cade swallowed hard as the full weight of his action settled over him. He had never turned his back on a commitment in his life, yet here he was, making promises he had no intention of keeping. It went against everything he knew to be right. The only thing that kept his feet firmly in place was the fact that the woman standing next to him was Belle.

"Until death do you part?"

A heartbeat, maybe two, lapsed before Cade answered in a clear voice, "I do."

"And do you, Margarite Isabella Farentino, take this man..."

Belle blinked back tears, determined not to let her emotions get out of hand. So, this wasn't the way she'd pictured her wedding day. So, it would have been wonderful to exchange vows with a man she truly loved. She would have her dream. And for a few short hours, Cade.

"Until death do you part?"

"I—I do."

"Then, by the power vested in me by the state of Texas, I now pronounce you man and wife. Go ahead, son. Kiss your bride," Overton urged.

As if he had been doing it for years, Cade pulled Belle into his arms and kissed her.

His lips didn't demand, but skillfully commanded hers to part and warm. With intense satisfaction he watched her lashes flutter and felt her sigh as he deepened the kiss.

Clutching the wrapped stem of her bouquet so hard her nails bit into her hand, she tried not to lean into the kiss. Tried to ignore the heat of it, the promise of more heat and the tingling awareness of danger. She was even moderately successful. But she suspected it was mainly because he ended the kiss before she tested her resolve. She felt slightly dizzy after his mouth left hers.

"Congratulations." Reese pumped Cade's hand, then gave Belle a peck on the cheek.

"Thanks." Belle tried to smile.

"Congratulations, you two." Sam Overton

grinned. "Now all you've got to do is sign the marriage license, and it's all legal."

Cade's hand was as steady as a rock as he signed his name in bold script. Belle was determined to be as detached as he was, and signed quickly, but she couldn't hold back a tremble or two.

Reese stepped up. "How 'bout I break out a bottle of merlot to toast the occasion? And I wouldn't be surprised if Posey hadn't baked a cake."

Cade looked at Belle. "You hungry?"

"No." She didn't dare ask him the same question. The look in his eyes was positively predatory, and she knew it had nothing to do with food.

"Thirsty?"

She shook her head.

"Guess we'll pass." Cade pointed to an overnight bag sitting by the coat tree. "That yours?"

"Yes. Thanks for everything, Reese," she said.

"Same goes for me." Cade opened the door, escorted his bride out, shook his friend's hand, and they were down the steps and into his truck.

"Always in a hurry, these newlyweds," Sam Overton observed as Cade backed the pickup out, turned around and took off, wheels spraying gravel like buckshot. "Where they headed?"

"Probably the first motel Cade comes to."

"EXACTLY WHERE ARE YOU taking me?"

"You'll see."

"All I see is an empty road and the night sky. There's not a hotel in sight."

"In a hurry?"

Belle didn't have to look at him to know he was grinning. She could feel it all the way over on her side of the truck. Her meager attempts at making conversation had backfired. She wasn't any good at small talk, and this situation was certainly not conducive to honing her skills. "No. I'm simply curious about our destination."

"Well, if it's a fancy hotel you're thinking of, I'm afraid you're in for a disappointment."

She wasn't thinking much of anything except that, in a short time, she and Cade would be...what? Consummating their deal? Making love? The latter was a lovely thought, but not very realistic. She sighed. "I suppose it doesn't matter. One place is as good as another."

"That's where you're wrong, darlin'." He whipped the pickup off the two-lane blacktop onto a gravel road. "It matters."

For the first time since he had decided on the location for their one and only night together, Cade was nervous. He was taking a big risk, and he knew it. One look and she might head for home without a backward glance.

"And I can promise you where we're going is like no place you've ever been before. It's got a great view. And it's private."

So private it was out in the middle of nowhere? They had been driving for more than twenty minutes, and Belle saw nothing in the beam of the truck's headlights but dusty road and mesquite trees. The lights of Lubbock could be seen over her right shoulder, but she couldn't even say for certain which direction they were traveling. Suddenly, he turned off the gravel road onto what could only be called a trail. He followed it for less than a quarter of a mile, then took a sharp right turn, down into what looked like a ravine, and came to a screeching halt. He killed the engine and lights.

"We're here."

Belle gazed out at...nothing. "Here, where?"

"Guess you could call it our honeymoon suite."

"If this is some kind of joke—"

"No joke, darlin'." Cade got out of the truck and immediately shed his coat. The best thing he could do was keep moving. If she had three seconds to think about any of this, she might insist he take her back to town, and he didn't want that. The few short hours they would have, he wanted completely private. "My terms, remember. I pick the place. No restrictions. No regrets."

"What does that have to do with the fact that we are out in the boonies in the middle of the night?"

He opened her door and offered his hand. "C'mon. Live dangerously."

"You're not going to tell me, are you?"

"Not yet."

Clueless about what he was up to, she had no choice but to go along with him. The sooner they were booked into a comfortable hotel room in town, the happier she would be. She set her bouquet on the seat, making sure none of the flowers would be crushed, then put her hand in his and slid out of the truck.

He took off into the darkness, pulling her along with him over uneven ground.

"Not so fast. And what about my bag?"

"You won't need it."

She could barely see where she was walking, and the three-inch heels on her white Italian leather pumps were definitely not made for trekking cross-country. "Cade, this is ridiculous. Where are we going?" They started up a steep hill, and she almost lost her footing. "And for the love of Pete will you please just slow—"

When they topped the hill Belle straightened, took a deep breath and almost forgot to release it.

At the bottom of the hill, some sixty yards ahead and silhouetted against a half-moon, was the biggest live oak tree she had ever seen in her life. It was huge, with enough foliage to shade two large houses. Beneath the tree, a small pile of logs surrounded by a neatly built ring of stones lay ready to be lit, and a few feet away were...

Two bedrolls. Unrolled. Side by side.

Belle stared at the campsite. Surely he couldn't mean for them to... He couldn't possibly intend to...

She turned to Cade, and the gleam in his eyes was all the confirmation she needed.

"You're not serious?"

"Don't I look serious?"

"Well, you're seriously insane if you think I'm going to sleep in one of those...those bedrolls."

"Who said anything about sleeping?"

She took a step back, then another. "No way." Finally she turned on her spindly heels, determined to find her way back down the hill to the truck.

He played his trump card and prayed. "So, I guess that means our deal is off. We both lose."

Belle stopped dead in her tracks and slowly turned to face him. She was going to get through this with as much dignity as possible, she vowed, even if it killed her. If he wanted to play home on the range, well...well, she would just have to live with it. She could handle anything for one night. Even Cowboy Cade. "No. A deal is a deal."

As Cade closed the distance between them, he realized he had been holding his breath for fear she might leave. Now that he was certain she would stay, he felt free to make tonight one they would never forget.

Moving in slowly, he slipped his hands around her waist and pulled her close. "Glad to hear it," he said as his lips brushed hers.

He took his time kissing her. Tasting her, really, his tongue exploring her softness like a connoisseur savoring the subtleness of a fine wine. Made in Italy, aged in Texas, she was a rare vintage. His hands spread over her narrow back, first stroking, then drawing her flush against his body.

She couldn't stop her breath from quickening any more than she could stop her heart from racing. His tongue teased hers, then made good on its offer, taking the kiss deeper, making erotic promises. For the first time in her life she knew the taste of desire. It was dark, slightly primitive, and totally thrilling. He was good at this. Better than good. And while her mind warned her she might be confusing expertise with real desire, her body wasn't interested in the finer points of such a debate. It only wanted to respond.

She pressed closer, her hands on his arms. Whether it was to keep herself from falling or to keep him from moving away, she couldn't say. And at the moment, she didn't care. To her chagrin, she actually moaned in protest when his mouth left hers.

"No need to rush, darlin'. We got all night."

All night. With Cade. With the raw desire she saw in the depths of his eyes, the strength she felt in his arms. Why did she suddenly feel as if she had just jumped off a cliff? And why wasn't she scared right down to the toes of her expensive shoes?

Oh, but she was scared.

And excited.

And the combination was more tantalizing than she had ever thought possible. Standing on a hilltop surrounded by splashes of moonlight and a million stars, in the arms of a man she had just married, yet barely knew, she felt a wildness sweep through her. A rush of yearning so strong it almost took her breath away. This hunger, this wildness, tasted like freedom. Pure, unbound liberation, shocking and exhilarating all at the same time. It came from the depths of her soul, dark and seductive. A mindless lust, a long-denied heritage.

And mixed with the desire she felt rushing through Cade, it was overwhelming. Too much to handle all at once. She had to regain control. But when she pulled away, she had the sensation she was breaking some kind of magnetic force field. "Where...where are we?" she whispered, surprised she had any power of speech at all.

Cade grinned. "Boy Scout camp."

Ten seconds later she was standing at the foot of the bedrolls and Cade was lighting the fire. "You made that up." She was trying to keep him at arm's length, emotionally as well as physically, but she had to admit the mental picture of him as a freckle-faced camper was charming, even endearing. "I just hope we're not trespassing on private property."

"My troop used to camp down here every summer for two weeks." He gave her the traditional salute. "Scout's honor. And we have all the comforts of home, including food and drink." He pointed to a cooler on the other side of the tree. "Even running water."

Sure enough, as her eyes adjusted to the darkness, she saw two springs, one close by, the other several yards distant. They gurgled over shadowed rocks, making a soothing sound.

"Looks like you thought of everything."

"We aim to please." He trailed a hand over her bare shoulder, then ran his fingertips along her lacy neckline. "I like your dress."

"Dress?" She blinked, slightly dazed, her heart racing at his touch. "Oh, yes. Thanks, I, uh, bought it in Italy." Pride prevented her from admitting that when she bought the dress, she'd dreamed of wearing it to their wedding. The man already had enough self-confidence to fill the state, he didn't need an ego booster.

"Silk?" His hand trailed down her arm, captured her fingers and lifted them to his lips.

"Hmm. Uh-huh."

He kissed her fingertips. "You look great in it."

"Th-thanks."

He nuzzled his way to her ear. "But I'm about to go crazy thinking about what you'll look like out of it." Then he kissed her again. His arms closed around her hard, and his tongue moved deep into her mouth, boldly staking his claim.

Belle's neck went back under the pressure, yet she

strained into the kiss as the wildness came roaring back, more powerful than before. So long suppressed, it now refused to be denied. It exploded inside her like a blast of sexual heat. The force of it whipped around her body, lashing away the last remnant of her thinly veiled control. The dark passion she had tasted earlier flowed from his body to hers, then back again. And once shared, that passion heightened, magnified. She wanted this. She needed this.

"Take it off," he ordered when they both finally came up for air.

There was no use pretending she didn't know what he wanted her to do. Cade was calling the shots, and she realized she didn't care. What good was control when they both wanted the same thing? A small voice in the back of her mind warned, yes, but not for the same reason. She deliberately ignored it. She started to turn her back on him as she reached for the zipper.

"No. I want to see you."

Holding his gaze, Belle reached around and pulled down the zipper. The lacy bodice drooped, then fell, leaving her bare to the waist. Panhandle nights were cool, and she should have shivered when a gentle breeze kissed her skin. Instead, she felt hot, almost fevered, as if she had been in the sun all day.

Judging from the style of the dress, he had surmised that she wasn't wearing a bra, and he was right. He also knew from holding her against him that her breasts were full, but he wasn't prepared for his own reaction. Already hard, his erection intensified to the point of being painful. It should have been a signal that he was in over his head, but he didn't notice. Just like his fascination with how the firelight made her skin glow should have been an indication of just how emotionally involved he was. He told himself this one time was the end, not the beginning. When he had possessed her, he would be free of whatever hold she'd had over him since that one hot kiss. Now she was his. No restrictions.

"Take it all off."

Belle kicked her shoes off, then pushed the dress over her hips. It fell, forming a pool of white lace around her ankles, and she stepped out of it wearing nothing but a garter belt, stockings and bikini panties. Still without breaking eye contact she unhooked one stocking front and back, raised her knee and began removing the stocking.

Cade could barely breathe, much less think. Where was his control? Where was his distance? Before he realized what he was doing, he was on his knees, throwing the discarded dress to one side. Holding her slender calf, he helped her free of the stocking. When he reached to undo the other one, she put her hand on his shoulder for balance. In seconds, her legs were as bare as her breasts, and she was clad in only the bikini panties. His hands slid up the outside of her thighs, leaving a trail of heat. He caressed her, moving his hands up and down her long, slender legs, each time going higher until he cupped her bottom. He smiled at her quick intake of breath.

Belle wasn't sure how much longer her legs would support her. They trembled with every touch, every stroke of his hands. In fact, her whole body was trembling, and it certainly wasn't from the cool night air. It was need. Desire, lust, call it whatever you wanted. She closed her eyes. All she knew was that she wanted his hands on her body. All over her body. She wanted his touch, his kisses. She wanted him.

He stroked her bottom, fitting his palms to her sweet roundness, then moved his hands up to her hips. Hooking his index fingers in the narrow waistband of the next-to-nothing panties, he pulled them down over her legs and off.

She gasped as he caught her behind the knees, making her legs give way. In an instant, they were knee to knee, eye to eye, lust to lust.

"Unbutton my shirt."

He didn't need to ask. Belle's hands were already halfway there. Her trembling fingers worked at the stubborn buttons with limited success. Frustrated, she looked to him for help. "They're stuck...my fingers—"

He grabbed his shirt just below the collar. "To hell with it." And with one furious yank, the buttons popped free like the last few kernels in a popcorn popper.

She pushed the shirt open, her hands eagerly gliding over his hard, warm flesh. When he shrugged free of the shirt, she continued her tantalizing exploration. It was difficult to say which one sighed first, but both sighs were of pure unadulterated pleasure.

The fact that he was as affected by her touching him as she was, fueled the wildness, stoked a boldness she hadn't known existed within her until tonight. Now she gave it free rein. "Touch me the way I'm touching you."

Cade blinked at her unexpected request. Had she just asked him to—

"I want to feel your hands on me."

Sweet heaven. He had no idea what had happened to the prim and proper Isabella, but for his money, this one was a damn sight more to his taste. From that first kiss, he had suspected her coolness was a veneer, and now he knew just how thin that veneer was. And the kind of heat that lay beneath it. He reached out and filled his hands with her hot, firm flesh.

She was like some erotic dream, sleek, smooth, and all her energy focused on one thing. Need. His, hers. The need they'd created together. The need that might be their undoing. But it was too late to turn back. No power on earth could prevent him from taking her now. When she arched her back, her breasts filling his hands, she made a sound that was part moan, part purr, and heat shot through him like a flash fire.

How could she have known this darkly passionate side of her would be so obsessive, so addictive? Even as the storm inside her built to the point of exploding, she still wanted more. Flesh to flesh. Heat to heat. Now. She wanted him now.

If he didn't have her soon, he'd go insane. It wasn't just a need to have sex, it was a need to possess. He'd never known this kind of hunger for a woman, and he was too far past control to do anything but let the hunger take him wherever it would. He hauled her against him, turning slightly so that his body would cushion hers as they fell onto the sleeping bags.

Frantic for the feel of all of him against all of her, she twisted in his arms, and her fingers tore at the snap of his pants.

"Hang on, darlin'." He reared up, and seconds later boots and pants went flying.

She had expected spectacular. She got magnificent. He was an extraordinary animal, and he was all hers. When he slipped his hands to her back and lifted her off the makeshift bed to his impatient lips, her fingers dug into his broad shoulders. His greedy mouth closed over her breast, and she sobbed his name.

The sound nearly drove him over the edge, and his hand slipped down to cover the source of her heat. Her body trembled, then quaked as he took her to first one peak, then another. Then when she was almost limp he pulled her beneath him.

She arched and took him deep, wrapping her legs around him.

She was moving under him like some wild thing, and all that kept him from going wild himself was his insatiable need for more of her. His mind was dark with lust as he plunged into her, angling her hips so that he could go as deep as her body would allow. Hard and deep.

They were lost in the heat, in each other, and all that mattered was the mind-robbing pleasure. It sucked them down, then tossed them up in an endless vortex, until finally they both simply let it take them. Over the moon. Over the edge.

She soared into a fulfillment so staggering it was both joy and pain, so pure she thought she might truly die of pleasure. Somewhere in the back of what still functioned as her brain whispered the thought, This is what it's like to be devoured by Cade McBride. Followed closely by the question, What would it be like to be loved by him?

# 3

PROPPED ON ONE ELBOW, Cade gazed down at his sleeping wife, her sweet little backside snuggled up to his front in a perfect fit. As he watched the gentle rise and fall of her breasts, he tried to figure out just exactly what had happened here an hour ago.

Something sure as hell had happened to him. And it wasn't just the sex thing. Not that it wasn't great. Hell, it was better than great. But sometime during all that great sex, things had changed. His feelings toward Belle had changed.

And Cade didn't like it one damn bit.

Women had always been easy for him. Some said too easy. Maybe so, but he never lied to a woman, contrary to the "love 'em and leave 'em" reputation some folks insisted was rightfully his. And because he didn't lie to the women he'd been with, didn't make promises he didn't intend to keep, sex had always been fun, and well...just sex. Granted, there had been a few along the way who were special, but none who held him for long.

Until now.

He'd never understood how entwined the body

and mind were, until this very moment. How intricate, complicated and unique that connection was. In one enlightening second, Belle had given him that connection like a precious gift.

But she had also taken something away.

His distance. His at-arm's-length protection. The fortress he had spent so many years building around his heart. In one heart-stopping second, she had given him more than he had ever thought possible, and taken away more than he could stand to lose.

Now he was a victim of his own need. The more he had her, the more he wanted her.

At some point, having sex had changed to making love, and he didn't even know when it had happened, only that it definitely had. Part of him was scared spitless at the mere thought of what this new development might mean. Another part gloried in the experience.

For all the good it would do him. His feelings might have changed, but in reality nothing else had. He had no more to offer her than he had three years ago.

Oh, hell, Cade thought. He couldn't afford to forget she was just a make-believe wife. They had an agreement. A business deal. They both got what they wanted. Belle would probably laugh out loud if she knew what he was thinking. It was just chemistry. That's all. Okay, so at the moment, he couldn't remember another woman satisfying him the way she had. In fact, he couldn't remember another woman, period. No woman had ever filled up his mind and senses so completely. Even now, he wanted her again.

His need was so deep, so urgent, he was almost afraid to touch her for fear he would yank her beneath him and pound himself into her. But when she stirred beside him, he couldn't *not* touch her.

"Cade?"

He ran his hand from her shoulder to her thigh and back up to her breast. "Right here, darlin'."

Eyes still closed, she gave a long, contented sigh. "You were wonderful."

"So were you."

She opened her eyes. "I've never felt anything like that. It was sort of scary and—"

"Exciting."

"Very."

"I've got to admit it was one wild ride."

"Then, I was okay?" The insecurity slipped out before she could stop herself. Great. Now he was going to think she was desperate for his approval, which was true no matter how much she hated to admit it. "I mean...I just wanted to be sure, you know, that you, uh—"

"Got everything that was coming to me?"

"Yes."

If someone had told him she could surprise him twice in one night, he probably would have called

them a bald-faced liar. But she had. First, the unexpected boldness when they made love, and now this.
The only label he found to describe the hesitancy in
her question was shyness. Was it possible she didn't
know that she was an incredibly sexy woman? This
vulnerability was a side of Belle he'd never seen. The
need to reassure her was too strong to ignore.

"I've never been with any woman who pleased me
more." It was the truth, and it scared him. "I love
those little sounds you make when I touch you. Sorta
like purring."

"The sound of satisfaction."

"Well, it makes me want to take you again. Right
now."

"Really? Can you? I mean—"

He rocked his hardness against her soft, smooth
belly. "What do you think?"

She blinked, heat flashing through her body. "I
think—I hope you're going to make love to me
again."

"You can count on it, darlin'."

In one smooth stroke he was deep inside her, but
this time there was no frenzy, no rush to climax. For
reasons he didn't want to examine too closely, he
wanted to pleasure her slowly, tenderly. He cher-
ished her breasts, kissing, suckling until her whole
body was drawn tight as a bow. Applying every bit of
expertise he had ever acquired, he made slow, sweet
love to her, wanting it to last. He watched her face, sa-

vored the beauty of each moment, at the same time not fully understanding why it was so important for him to do so.

And when she whispered endearments in his ear, his spirit flew, his heart flooded with joy. When the time drew near, he kissed her deeply, passionately, heightening not only her need, but his own. Still, he wanted it to go on forever. It was a sensation he had never experienced, and didn't quite know how to handle. It was too overpowering, too entwined with this woman. Perhaps that was why when he finally poured himself into her, he felt something break free inside him, and then he felt empty clear to his soul. Finally, gratefully, there was only exhaustion and sleep.

As Belle felt Cade's body relax, the tears she had fought hard to control rolled down her cheeks. Why couldn't he have turned out to be the cad she thought he was? Why did he have to be so exciting, so tender, so...so all the things she wanted? All the promises she had made to herself not to let him get too close, not to risk another heartbreak, had vanished with his tenderness.

For all the good it would do her. She still wasn't the kind of woman he wanted for more than one night.

THERE WAS ONLY a faint tinge of pink on the horizon when Cade roused a sleepy-eyed Belle.

"Cade?"

"Hang on, darlin'. We're going home." While she slept, he had transformed the joined sleeping bags back into individual ones, scattered the ashes from the fire, loaded the cooler and packed her clothes into the back of the truck.

"But it's still night."

"For about thirty more minutes, then the sun's going to turn this bag into a sauna. It's supposed to be in the triple digits today."

Still naked, Belle gasped when he scooped her into his arms, bag and all, and started walking toward where they had left his truck.

"What are you doing?"

They topped the hill where he'd kissed her the first time last night and started down. "Taking you home."

"I can't go home like this." She clutched the edge of the sleeping bag.

"Now, don't go all prissy on me."

"But Cade—"

"After last night, you couldn't sell that attitude if it was studded with diamonds."

They were now at the truck, and he opened the driver's door and plopped her onto the seat.

"If you'd let me finish, you would have heard me say, I don't want to go home."

His gaze drilled hers. "So, roughing it wasn't so bad, after all?"

She ran her hand over his stubbled cheek. "Funny, but I've discovered I rather like roughing it."

He hauled her against him and kissed her so hard she couldn't breathe, much less talk. His mouth was hot and hungry, and it evoked delicious memories of the night they'd spent together. Instinctively, her arms wound around his neck to draw him closer. He wasn't wearing a shirt, and touching his skin sent tremors of excitement through her.

"Hmm." She kissed his collarbone, his throat, ran her tongue along his jaw.

Cade's body tightened. "Just hang on, baby." He scooted her over, slid beneath the wheel and they were off.

With one arm still around his neck, Belle yawned, snuggling as close to him as she could get, which wasn't nearly close enough considering the bulky bedding surrounding her. She couldn't believe what they had done, what *she* had done last night. And the doing was nothing compared to the feelings that went with it. The first time had been hot and fast, but the second... The second time she had whispered things to him. Loving things. She hadn't even realized at the time that she had opened her heart.

Being with Cade was like being awakened from a long, dark sleep. She felt vibrant, full of energy. Alive. He was the best thing that had ever happened to her. How ironic that it had taken a marriage made in a lawyer's office for her to discover the treasure that had been only a stone's throw away. What they had shared had nothing to do with the winery or land. It had to do with connecting with another person, with intimacy. The kind she had only dreamed about. But the time in Cade's arms was no dream. It did, however, pose a question.

Had he felt the magic, too?

He must have felt something to have been so tender and, dare she say it, loving. And if he had, was there something more for them than their "deal"?

The answer to that question depended on whether he really cared about her. Could he make love to her as he had and feel nothing for her?

Then she caught sight of her wedding bouquet. Smiling, she picked up the flowers and carefully tucked them inside the bag, next to her heart. Sending the flowers was a small but romantic gesture, and it thrilled her. Just the thought that he had wanted her to have them, wanted to make their wedding as nice as he could even under the unusual circumstances almost made her cry. Another tenderness. Another sign that maybe there was more for them? It definitely gave her hope. As she slipped back into sleep, she made a mental note to tell him how much she appreciated such an endearing gesture.

What seemed like only seconds later, he roused her, and she again found herself being carried in his arms. She could get used to this, she thought sleepily. He unlocked the door, then carried her straight into

her darkened bedroom and all but tossed her on the
bed. She was about to protest his rough treatment
when she heard him turn the lock.

"What are you doing?"

"Thought you weren't ready for this night to end."

"I'm not." Her heart was already racing, her body
humming with sweet anticipation.

"We wouldn't want anybody to walk in on us,
now, would we?"

"And what would they see if they did?"

Her answer was the rasp of zippers. His, and the
sleeping bag's. Cool air whispered over her skin a
moment before his heated touch stroked the inner
softness of her calf, her thigh.

"They'd get an eyeful."

"Like I am?"

He reached for her. "Hell, I don't care if they take a
picture of me buck naked and publish it in the *Sweetwater Springs Gazette*, but I'm not too wild about
somebody gawking at your sweet little fanny."

It was a totally macho, "you're-my-woman" kind
of thing to say, and Belle's heart beat even harder.
The undercurrent of wildness still swirled and ebbed
within her, and the hunger rose, but something had
been added. A deeper yearning she hadn't even
known was there until tonight.

"Speaking of wild..." She curled her fingers in his
hair and pulled his mouth to hers for a ravenous kiss.

"You're going to break me at this rate. No wonder

men run from marriage like a spooked jackrabbit. I had no idea how demanding a wife could be."

She nibbled her way from his lips to his earlobe. "You ain't seen nothing yet."

He rolled over, positioning her on top of his body. "I can't wait. You're about to drive me—"

"Oh, be careful."

"Darlin', I'm always careful."

"No, silly." She tugged on his shoulder. "Get up. You're on my bouquet." She lifted the slightly smushed flowers from beneath his broad shoulder.

"You're thinking of daisies at a time like this? They're gonna die, anyway."

"It's my wedding bouquet. And they're roses. I can't believe your attitude. First you give me these gorgeous flowers, then you act as if you could care less."

"I don't. And what makes you think I sent them?"

"Well, of course you did. Reese said he was delivering them personally from you."

"Darlin', I hate to disappoint you, but I didn't send you roses or daisies or any other kind of flower."

"You didn't?"

He ran his hands over her naked backside. "Nope."

"Well, then who—"

"If I had to guess, I'd say Reese."

"Reese?"

"Yeah. It's his style."

And it was, Belle realized. Cade hadn't thought about a bride, even a make-believe one, needing or wanting a bouquet. His friend had covered for him. It was a small thing, but it was hurtful. More hurtful than she could ever have imagined.

He nuzzled her neck. "Why are we talking about Reese and some silly flowers when we could be talking about much more important things? Like the fact that you've got the most gorgeous mouth I've ever tasted."

Belle stared at the rumpled roses and flattened baby's breath. Flattened, like her hope. She shivered, suddenly cold. What a fool she had been. She had actually entertained thoughts of them together. For real. She meant no more to him than the hundreds of other women he'd made love to. Correction. He'd had sex with.

"And you would know, wouldn't you?"

"What does that mean?"

She slid off him, feeling stripped bare and exposed in a way that had nothing to do with the fact that she was unclothed. In her pain, the need to lash out at him was so strong she could actually taste the bitterness.

"It just means that you're the expert on mouths and kisses and...everything. Aren't you?"

Cade wasn't exactly sure what had happened in the past few seconds, but she was clearly ticked off.

"I've had my share of kisses. And *everything*. But that's not exactly a news flash."

"No. I guess I just...forgot that for a moment."

Belle had perfected her own kind of expertise. After years of practice, she had become so deft at glossing over her pain and disappointment with anger that it was second nature. She reached for that expertise now like a lifeline.

"So..." She scooted to the other side of the bed and grabbed her robe, pulling it around her body, the same way she had learned to pull a protective shield around her heart. "How was I? I mean, on a scale of one to ten, where do I rate?"

"Rate? I don't know what's got you so riled, but—"

"I'm not riled," she lied. "Just curious."

"You want me to tell you how you stack up against other women I've—"

"Why not?"

"Do I look like I'm crazy? That's a female question if ever I heard one. And no man in his right mind would try to answer it. That alone is proof you're riled."

She jumped off the bed and spun around to face him. "I'm not riled!"

"Could have fooled me."

"That's no great achievement."

Cade sat up, ran his fingers through his hair and tried to figure out how everything had fallen apart so fast. If he didn't know better, he'd think she was de-

liberately picking a fight. "Look, I'm sorry I didn't
send the damn flowers. Is that what you wanted to
hear?"

God, what an idiot she had been. How could she
have let her guard down like this? How could she
have forgotten for one moment that this night was
part of their deal? Nothing more. And she had no one
to blame but herself.

"Hey, you never promised me a rose garden." It
was trite, but she didn't care.

No doubt about it. She was goading him into a
fight. Well, he wasn't going to take the bait, no matter
what she said. "No. I didn't. But up until a few moments ago I thought we were having a real good
time."

"You certainly were."

"I didn't hear you complain. Either time."

Pride rose up in her, hot and thick, blinding her to
reason. All she could think about were the loving
words she had whispered to him. The long-held passion she had so freely given. How had she fallen so
quickly and easily, when she knew what kind of man
he was? Well, she might have made a fool of herself
last night, but now it was broad daylight. No longer
was she an easy mark. No longer a pushover. And
she was fully capable of doing a little pushing herself.

"There was nothing to complain about. You were
perfectly acceptable."

"Acceptable?" Dammit to hell, she'd gone too far.

After all, a man had his pride. "I noticed you were pretty damned *accepting* when the time came."

She reached behind her, grabbed the sash to her robe and yanked it tight around her waist. Her cheeks were hot with barely leashed anger, and her whole body trembled. "You are no gentleman."

He was out of the bed in a flash, jerking on his jeans. "It wasn't a gentleman you were looking for last night, and we both know it. You wanted me as bad as I wanted you. And you wanted me the same way I wanted you. Hot, fast and deep." He yanked on his socks, then shoved his feet into his boots. "You just don't have the guts to admit it."

He wanted guts. She'd show him guts. "You've had your one night, Mr. McBride. I want you to leave."

"It can't be fast enough to suit me." As calmly as if he had all day, he picked up his hat, settled it on his head and gave her a wicked grin. "Pleasure doing business with you, ma'am."

Belle's control snapped. "And don't come back."

He reached for his shirt. "What?"

"You heard me. Don't come back. You're—you're fired."

"You can't do that. We've got a deal."

"There's nothing in our agreement that states you're guaranteed employment. Don't worry, you'll get your deed. In twelve months, have your lawyer contact mine, and they'll work out the transfer."

"Meanwhile, I'm out of a job." Her careless shrug was like waving a red flag at a bull. Anger seethed and bubbled within him, showing all the potential of a volcano on the verge of erupting. "I got pay coming. I want it now."

"Call the bookkeeper later today. He'll cut you a check." With that she stalked out of the bedroom.

Cade was hot on her heels, following her into the very room where they had sealed their deal less than six days ago. "No way. You want me gone, hand over the money. Four hundred and fifty dollars a week plus two weeks' severance."

"Severance! Not on your life."

"I figure it comes to thirteen hundred and fifty." He walked around the mahogany desk. "And don't tell me you don't keep that kind of cash around because I know different."

"That's blackmail, and I'm not paying it. Don't touch anything!" she yelled when he reached for one of the drawers.

He walked back around and took a step toward her. "Why, you little piker. I ought to turn you over my knee and paddle your butt."

She backed away, but he had her trapped between him and the natural stone fireplace that covered one wall of the study. "You wouldn't dare."

"Oh, darlin'. Don't ever dare a man who's got very little to lose. As a matter of fact, I think you could use a good spanking."

"Don't try it," she warned, ready to sprint past him at the first opportunity. "I mean it, Cade. You lay one finger on me, and I'll—I'll..."

"You'll what?"

"I'll call the police."

He grinned. "I can just see the headlines now. Winery Heiress in Domestic Dispute. Great for business."

The fact that he wasn't even taking her rage seriously made Belle that much more determined for him not to win. She leaned to the right, then in a flash switched direction, faking him out. She dashed across the room, down the hall and into the wide foyer, the rap of his boots on the hardwood floor ringing in her ears. He grabbed for her arm, but she jerked free. When she tried to run, he blocked her path, backing her up against the gun cabinet along one wall of the foyer.

"Now, just calm down."

Belle needed to get him out of her house. Every minute he stayed was more humiliation. Worse, she recognized that wicked gleam in his eyes. He knew her weaknesses now. All of them. Anger and pride notwithstanding, if he got close enough to kiss her, she was a goner.

"Okay." She held out a hand. "Okay, I guess I, uh, got a little carried away."

"That temper of yours is going to get you into trouble one of these days."

Belle took a deep breath, willing herself to at least appear calm. "So I've been told."

Cade relaxed. "Now, maybe we can talk sensibly."

Sensibly? It hadn't been Belle who'd been acting like the town bully. She wanted to smack him so hard his teeth would rattle. Most of all, she wanted him gone, whatever it took.

"First, would you bring in my overnight bag? Please."

The request was unexpected, but at least it was reasonable. "I'll be right back." He pointed his finger at her. "Then we're going to talk."

When she heard him step off the front porch, she locked the door.

Cade retrieved the bag, along with the rest of her things, then headed up the steps. He slung the white lace dress under one arm and tried to turn the knob.

"Belle? Open this door."

"No."

"Dammit, Belle. I look like a fool standing out here holding all this lace...and stuff."

All he cared about was how foolish he looked. Couldn't he see how he had hurt her? Couldn't he understand that she just wanted him to leave her alone?

"Go away, Cade."

"Not until I talk to you. Open this door."

He was only making everything worse. She *had* to make him leave.

"I mean it, Belle. Right now or I swear I'll kick it down."

When she didn't answer, he tried one last time. "I'm counting to three. One...two..." The door swung open. "Now, that's more—"

She stood in the doorway pointing a .22 caliber pump-action rifle at him. "You got the down payment on our deal. You get the rest in twelve months. Until then, I don't want to see your worthless hide on my property."

The wad of frothy lace slipped from beneath his arm as he carefully set the overnight bag on the porch. "This isn't funny, Belle. Put that thing away before you get hurt."

For the life of him, he didn't understand how they had gone from great sex to guns, but he did understand that somehow it was his fault. And that she was serious. He also knew she had been around guns and horses all her life and could handle both.

"Back away, Cade." He did. "And keep going until you're off Farentino land."

"I'm going."

He walked to his truck and opened the door, then stopped. This was insane. They were both acting irrationally. He slammed the truck door.

"I don't know what's got you so uptight, but I'm not leaving here until we—"

The first shot struck not three feet from where he stood. "Dammit, Belle!" He jumped into the truck and closed the door. When he heard her pump the rifle a second time, he cursed, started the engine and took off.

Belle waited until his pickup disappeared through the gate before she slumped against the open doorway. From the back of the house, she could hear Posey running to see what was going on. She stepped back inside and quickly wiped the tears from her cheeks. Cade McBride was out of her life.

# 4

HE'D MADE SOME MISTAKES in his life, but this one had to be, bar none, his all-time personal worst. No question about it. If there was a Jerk of the Year award, he would be the hands-down winner. The weathered sign stating he was entering Sweetwater Springs, Texas, and proclaiming it to be the oasis of the panhandle, materialized out of the dark into the glare of his headlights, then swept back into the night as his pickup truck approached the outskirts.

And as if being a first-class jerk wasn't bad enough, he was going back for seconds.

Who would have ever thought that he, Cade McBride, would be hog-tied over a woman? It wasn't his style. Hell, he hadn't even thought it was possible until six weeks ago. But that was before he'd married a dark-eyed, dark-haired beauty with a head for business, and the body and soul of a gypsy enchantress. He had known a lot of women, but none of them had ever gotten to him the way Belle had.

Memories of the way she smelled, the way she walked, the softness of her skin, haunted him. And the harder he tried to push the memories away, the more vivid they became. They filled his waking thoughts and dominated his dreams. He was alone even in a crowd, and miserable with his own company. Despite all his self-denial to the contrary, he knew Belle was the cause. Just like he knew that, in one night, he had gotten in way over his head.

She was under his skin, part of his soul. And it had taken him weeks to admit the truth to himself. That he was afraid he had fallen for her despite all his efforts to the contrary.

It probably began the first time he kissed her almost three years ago, and he was too blind to see it. Cade McBride, nutty over Isabella Farentino. Wasn't that a kick in the butt. No, not Farentino. McBride. She was his wife. And the marriage had been consummated.

Brother, had it ever. One long, hot night that had kept him practically dancing on the edge of insanity ever since. He had never known a woman who could leave him so dazed and weak-kneed.

Cade shifted his position behind the wheel and tried to adjust his suddenly too-tight jeans, but it didn't work. Nothing worked when he thought about Belle. Not cold showers. Not booze. Not even other women.

And he had tried them all.

The showers and the booze to excess. But it had taken only one time with another woman to make him realize that the freewheeling, "love 'em and leave 'em" Cade was a thing of the past. He hadn't even had the heart to finish the so-called seduction. It had taken him only a few minutes to realize the well-built, blue-eyed buckle bunny in his arms was a poor substitute for the woman he really wanted.

He couldn't stop thinking about Belle. And more disturbing was wondering whether or not she was pregnant. It was certainly possible. He'd had every intention of using protection that night, but she had surprised him with all that unexpected fire. He had always been so careful, but before he knew it, things had gone too far, too fast. Then it had been too late.

What if she was carrying his child right now?

Before marrying Belle, the idea of becoming a father would have scared him right down to his boots, and to some degree, it still did. But it also pleased him. So much so, that he had to admit he would be more than a little disappointed if she wasn't pregnant. And if she was, he was not above adding her condition to his arsenal of weapons. He didn't like the idea of bullying her into taking him back, but he was prepared to do just that, because he knew it was the only way he could get the answer to the question that had plagued him ever since he left Texas. Was he merely suffering from a fatally wounded ego, or was he in love with Belle?

Granted, they might have put the cart before the horse, so to speak, but stranger things had happened. He had spent so much time telling himself she was out of his reach, he wasn't sure exactly what he was feeling. And he intended to find out.

Cade whipped the truck into the parking lot of the first decent-looking motel he saw, got a room and unloaded the small duffel bag he had retrieved from the front seat of his truck. He needed a shower and a good night's sleep. Tomorrow he would see Belle and find out if she was carrying his child. Once he saw her, maybe his thoughts wouldn't be so muddled. And if the feelings keeping him awake nights turned out to be the real thing, he knew he had to act on them.

Cade sighed. If he was in love with Belle, nothing about it was going to be easy. He had hurt her, wounded her pride. Something he knew all about. But thanks to his friend Logan Walker and some long talks over a lot of long-neck bottles of beer, he now knew at least one place he had gone wrong and had a plan to correct the situation.

A plan that didn't include sex.

Over the past several weeks while he'd stayed with Logan in Denver, he had done a lot of thinking about the night he and Belle had shared. And he had finally come to the conclusion that their libidos were definitely barriers to their well-guarded hearts. Speaking for himself, as long as he had been able to keep his need for Belle strictly physical, he didn't have to deal with the emotional part. He had a hunch that went double for Belle. So, they wanted each other, and that was fine. But they had let their bodies, and all that deliciously hot sex, get in the way.

Well, the times, they were a-changin'. This time he intended to do things right. Too much was at stake not to. She wasn't going to be happy to see him, that much was certain. But he was convinced he could change her mind.

So convinced, in fact, that everything he had was riding on it, including his heart.

ALVIN DELLWORTHY CROSSED the street in front of the hardware store, making a beeline for the gathering of tobacco-chewing, wood-whittling senior citizens of Sweetwater Springs who spent their days, weather permitting, on benches beneath the one-hundred-year-old oak tree on the courthouse square. He stepped up over the foot-high curb and didn't slow his steps until he was smack-dab in front of them.

"Cade McBride's back in town," he announced, a little winded from keeping up his brisk pace in order to be the first one to reach them with the news.

"The hell you say." The man who had been called just Old Walt for so long some people couldn't remember his last name, didn't even look up as he spoke. He just kept whittling on his current project, a coiled rattlesnake. "Didn't figure he'd ever show his face in this town again after what he done."

"Is he alone?" toothless Smitty Lewis asked.

"It's him for sure," Alvin said, hardly missing a

beat. "Seen him myself over at the Texaco station not a half hour ago."

"What you reckon he's up to?"

"Sure he was by himself?" Smitty asked insistently. "Always had an eye for the ladies, that one. Lookers, too. Liked big chests, and legs clean up to who'd thought it. Bet he had a woman with him."

"Same thing he was up to when he left here. No good." Alvin pushed his straw cowboy hat back on his head. "You figure Belle knows?"

"If she don't, probably won't be long 'fore she gets word. News like this ain't gonna sit still, and that's a fact."

Smitty grinned his empty smile. "There musta been a woman inside the station waitin' for him. You jest weren't lookin'."

"When Reese hears, I figure all hell's gonna break loose."

"You can take that to the bank."

"Hellfire, Alvin, ain't you gonna answer me?" Smitty demanded. "Did he have a woman with him or not?"

Finally Alvin turned to Smitty. "Cade McBride may be crazy, but he's not stupid. You really think he's gonna show up with some flashy woman on his arm? Belle would probably shoot him on sight."

"That's 'xactly what she did the last time she saw him," Smitty reminded both men.

"She didn't hit him. That old .22 of her granddaddy's ain't worth the powder it would take to blow it to hell."

"Wasn't for lack of tryin', I hear."

"Uh-oh. Look over yonder." The other two turned to follow the direction of Old Walt's bony finger. Across the street, Reese Barrett, assistant manager of the Farentino Winery, was entering the Sweetwater Springs Café.

Still gazing at the café, Alvin resettled his hat on his head. "You know, a cup of hot coffee sure sounds good."

Old Walt's aged bones creaked as he stood. "I reckon I could use another cup." He snapped the blade back into his pocketknife.

"Had three cups already," Smitty said. "But I got to whiz somethin' fierce."

Together, the men walked across the street and into the café. Reese was sitting at the counter reading the newspaper.

A fresh-brewed pot of coffee in hand, Rubydell Bookbinder watched the three men amble in and knew exactly what was on their minds. Clive Mooney from the Texaco station had been in less than twenty minutes ago with the hottest piece of gossip to hit town in months. A few minutes after Clive left, Reese had walked in. It didn't take a rocket scientist to see what Alvin, Smitty and Old Walt were up to.

"Hey there, Reese. How's it goin'?"

Reese looked up from his paper and nodded to the

three in turn. "Alvin. Old Walt. Hey, Smitty. What you boys up to?"

"Not much," Alvin said, taking the lead. "Say, uh, guess you're about fit to be tied over the news."

"What news is that?"

"You ain't heard?"

"No, but I'll bet you're dying to tell me, Smitty."

"We sure hate to be the ones to spring it on you, Reese." Old Walt ran a hand over his stubbled chin. "And that's a fact."

AT & T had nothing on Sweetwater Springs, Texas, when it came to passing on news. And these three men were the holy trinity of tattle.

Reese put down his newspaper. "All right, let's have it."

"Cade McBride's back in town."

FORTY-FIVE MINUTES LATER, Belle paced in front of the massive mahogany desk that had once been her grandfather's. "You're sure?" she asked Reese.

"Alvin Dellworthy saw him at the Texaco station. Guess that classifies as an eyewitness report."

"Great! If Alvin, Old Walt and Smitty know, then the whole town is talking about it!"

Leaning against the open study door, Reese watched Belle pace. She was in fine form, he thought. He'd never seen her more irate, or more beautiful. Cade ought to have his head examined for walking out on her.

"You would think," she went on, "that the man would have the common decency to—" She threw up her hands. "What am I saying? Cade McBride and common decency are polar opposites. Oh, he's got some nerve showing his face around here. I have never been so humiliated—"

"If I were him," Reese said, shoving his Stetson back on his head, "I'd think twice about calling on a woman who fired a rifle at me the last time I saw her."

"I didn't fire *at* him."

Reese grinned. "My mistake."

Belle stopped pacing and turned to looked at him. "Are you taking his side?"

He held up both hands in a gesture of surrender. "Do I look like a fool? Besides, Cade doesn't need anyone to take his side. Never has. Never will. And unless I miss my guess, he'd resent the hell out of anyone who tried."

"The man is insufferable."

"He's also your husband."

"Don't remind me."

"I think, Mrs. McBride, that is exactly the point. You are married to Cade. And at the risk of damaging our friendship, not to mention losing my job, may I remind you that it was all your idea?"

"A business arrangement, pure and simple," she told him. But she was careful to turn away, hoping that her expression didn't betray the conflicting emotions she'd been experiencing ever since she heard Cade had returned.

Why? she asked herself. "He rode out of here without a backward glance. Why—"

"Ask him."

"I will not!"

Reese pushed away from the door. "Lord, save me from a stubborn woman," he mumbled.

"What?"

"Nothing."

"What if he's decided to get back at me for that...that gun thing? You don't think he's come back to ask for a divorce, do you?"

"McBride never went back on a deal in his life. I know people say he's shiftless, but they don't know him. When Cade makes a promise, or a commitment, he doesn't break it. Ever. I've got a feeling your problem is more serious."

"Well then, what on earth is he doing back in Sweetwater Springs?"

Reese shrugged, then headed for the front door. "I've got work to do."

"No, wait. I need you to help me—"

"Gotta go." Without looking back or breaking his stride he opened the door and left.

"Traitor," she called after him, squelching the urge to stomp her foot. What was it about Cade McBride that reduced her to childishness?

Belle flipped a wave of hair back over her shoulder.

She would not do this again. She was an intelligent, levelheaded woman, and under most circumstances, congenial and flexible.

But not with Cade.

Every time he crossed her path, her usual poise and grace went out the window. More appropriately, went up in smoke. She lost her cool. Never in her life had she met anyone like him. And never in her life had she reacted to anyone as she did to Cade.

Maybe that was because no one had ever hurt her the way he had.

With a sigh, Belle sat down in her grandfather's chair. She wondered what he would think of the mess she had made of her life. Running her fingers over the chair's soft leather arms, she thought about the absurd stipulation in his will and wished she had just ignored it. But if she had, she might have lost her dream.

And the only obstacle standing between her and her dream was six feet two inches of broad-shouldered, hardheaded cowboy.

Cade McBride was lethal where women were concerned. But Belle had learned her lesson. Oh, brother, had she. One night with him was enough for her. One night together, then she got her dream, and he got his, only...

It hadn't turned out the way she'd expected. In fact, even now his legacy of erotic dreams still robbed her of sleep. Dreams in which she relived that primitive night of passion and the unexpected tenderness that had left her shaken to her core.

She had been prepared for the passion. But the gentleness Cade displayed had completely undone her. So much so, that in the hours before dawn, still in his embrace, she had wept because it wasn't real.

But her emotions had been real enough. They still were, no matter how hard she tried to deny them. Cade had touched her physically, emotionally, even spiritually. He had shown her what real passion was, not to mention the fact that sex could be fun. She wasn't a virgin, but after one soaring trip over the moon with Cade, she had realized that her previous experience had not only been limited, but woefully inadequate. Cade met her on equal terms, as eager for her pleasure as his own. He encouraged, wooed and petted her until she thought she would die from pleasure. Then he took her higher. And all the while, he let her set the pace. Let her make her own discoveries about him, and herself. What she discovered was that sometime during that incredible night, she had fallen a little bit in love with him. She had awakened with stars in her eyes and romantic notions filling her head.

And then made a complete fool of herself.

Those damned flowers. If only she hadn't made such a big deal out of the fact that he hadn't sent them to her. If only she hadn't lost her temper. If only her pride hadn't gotten in the way.

Pride, her grandmother had often warned, would be her undoing. And she had been so right.

The minute she realized she had gone weak in the knees for a man who only saw her as a means to an end, she couldn't put up barriers between them fast enough. Cade hadn't sent her flowers. He hadn't whispered sweet words; she had. She had allowed passion to rule, and now she was paying the price. In a way, she had been as humiliated by her own behavior as she had at learning their night together hadn't meant anything to him.

But she didn't blame Cade. Well, maybe a little. Okay, a lot, at first, anyway. Then, after she'd had a chance to cool down, she realized he had never given her any reason to think there could be anything between them but their arrangement. All the fantasizing had been hers. Well, she should have known better. Once again, passion had left her abandoned. Only this time, she had no one to blame but herself.

And now Cade was back.

But why? The only answer that occurred to Belle was that he wanted out of their arrangement. It certainly couldn't be because he missed her.

"Yeah, right," she whispered.

Just then, she heard footsteps on the hardwood floor. "Is that you, Posey?" she called out to the cook.

"I've been called a lot of things in my life, but never a posy."

Belle shot out of the chair and whipped around to

find her husband standing just inside the doorway, carrying his saddle and tack.

"Hello, darlin'." He swung his saddle down off his shoulders. It landed with a thud on the floor. "I'm home."

"Y-y-you..." She couldn't seem to get her tongue in the correct position to form the right words. "Y-you're not supposed to be here," she finally managed to say.

"Now, darlin', is that any way to talk to your husband?"

"Y-you said you were never coming back."

"No, *you* told me not to come back."

"You broke your promise."

Cade shook his head. "Changed my mind." He started toward her. "There's a difference."

Completely rattled by his presence, she needed time to think. "I want...want you to leave. Right now."

He kept coming. "Too bad."

She took a step back. "But you can't just come in here and—"

"I sure can. We're married, remember."

She backed up several more steps. "In name only."

"Now, darlin', that's a Texas-size lie if I ever heard one, and you know it."

Belle took another step back and found herself up against the edge of the desk. "But—"

Cade closed the short distance between them in a

flash. He was so close she could almost feel his denim-clad legs against hers. "We got a whole new set of rules. I'm home, and I'm moving in."

She couldn't believe what she was hearing.

"And unless you want to call it quits right now and give up your dream, there's not much you can do about it. That's the new deal, darlin'. Take it or leave it."

He turned, walked to the door, then walked right back. "Oh, yeah. One more thing." He hauled her into his arms, all but lifting her off her feet as he gave her a hard, staggeringly deep kiss.

She told herself it was shock that had her struggling for breath. And a simple craving to be touched that had her fighting the urge to throw her arms around his neck and pull him closer. She knew this was a big mistake, one she would regret. But once again, her body paid little attention to her brain. Hating herself, but unable to stop, she melted against him like hot fudge over vanilla ice cream.

Cade had to bridle the urge to deepen the kiss. Hell, he had to summon all his willpower not to take her right here on the floor. For an instant, the mental image of them tangled in a sweaty heap almost snapped his resolve and sent his plan out the window. But then he remembered her pride. He would never win her heart by conquering. He wanted her body *and* soul.

He ended the kiss and set her away from him. It was pure self-preservation on his part. "Like I said, I'm back. Get used to it."

# 5

CADE MCBRIDE MAY HAVE stomped back into her life, but he wasn't going to stomp on her heart. Not again.

Dressed in white linen slacks and matching shell, and a navy linen blazer with a sterling silver replica of the Farentino logo pinned to the lapel, Belle surveyed her image in the mirror. Silver earrings dangled from her ears, her eyes were clear, her expression calm. Satisfied she was as well put together emotionally as she was physically, she was ready to face the day.

And Cade.

For the time being, it appeared there was nothing she could do to get rid of her houseguest, which was how she chose to think of him. He had moved in last night, taking the bedroom next to hers. For one heart-stopping moment when he'd paused at the doorway to her room, she thought he was taking up his conjugal rights as well as residence. But he just smiled, then moved on.

She knew what he was up to. He was probably convinced he was so charming, so sexy, that eventually she'd fall all over herself to get at him. He must have assumed that living in the same house would be too strong a temptation for her to resist. Now that he knew her weaknesses, he was probably planning to exploit them to his advantage.

Well, he was in for a surprise.

She *could* resist him. What was so irresistible about a man who was so disgustingly sure of himself, anyway? A cowboy who smelled of dust and horses. And sunshine. And leather. A little honest sweat mixed with a dash of—

Oh, no. She was not going to do this. What she *was* going to do was set her attorney on the trail of finding some way to get Cade out of her house and her life without losing the winery. Starting today, that was priority number one. She flicked a speck of lint from the shoulder of her blazer and headed downstairs.

"Good morning, darlin'."

He was at the kitchen table, his feet propped up on one of the chairs, a coffee mug in one hand.

When Belle shot him a cool glance, Posey, the cook and housekeeper, suddenly decided she had pressing duties elsewhere. After casually pouring herself a cup of coffee, Belle sat down at the opposite end of the table and picked up the newspaper.

"You're going to have to talk to me sooner or later."

She didn't answer him.

"Suit yourself. But you're going to get mighty tired of talking to yourself for the next ten months."

"If you're around that long," she said without looking up from her reading.

"Don't worry yourself. I'll be around."

Belle put down the newspaper and looked straight at him. "I think you should know that I'm meeting with my attorney this morning to find some way to get rid of you. If you were any kind of gentleman—"

"Thought we settled that issue the night we got married."

She opened her mouth to say something, then closed it. He was trying to rattle her nerves, but she refused to give him the satisfaction. Why don't you just leave?"

"Can't. No job, no place to go."

"Go back to wherever you've been for the past month and a half."

"Can't. My friend's lease was up. Had to move to a smaller place."

"Oh, I'm sure she'll make room for you."

Cade grinned. She thought he'd been with another woman, and it was gnawing at her. "Doubt it. I told Logan he was crazy to buy a one-bedroom trailer, but he wouldn't listen. So, you see, your poor husband is homeless."

Belle folded the paper and set it aside. "If it's money you want—" she carried her untouched cup of coffee to the sink "—I'm sure we can come to some kind of—"

Cade was out of his chair and across the kitchen in

a flash. He grabbed her by the shoulders and turned her around to face him. "Money isn't what I want from you."

He was so close she could see the flecks of gold in his hazel eyes. So close she could feel the fly of his jeans pressed against her. "Then what...what do you—"

"For one thing—" he leaned away from her just far enough to slide his hand over her tummy "—I want to know if you're pregnant."

Belle gasped. "Pregnant?"

"It's possible. I intended to use protection, but everything happened so fast."

How well she remembered. Until that moment she hadn't even considered the possibility that she might be pregnant. Oh, Lord, was she?

"Well, are you?"

"I can't think when you're hounding me."

"Well, think. It's important."

"I know that. I—I..."

"When was your last period?"

"None of your business."

"It damn sure is my business. If you're carrying my baby—"

"Stop saying that. I'm not pregnant!"

"Are you sure?"

No, she wasn't, but if she gave him even a hint of uncertainty, she knew he would badger her until he found out the truth. And she needed the truth before she could face him with it.

"Yes. Now, will you leave me alone?" She shoved him away and ran from the kitchen.

Cade had often thought about what it would be like if Belle was carrying his child and how he would handle the situation. But he had never considered how he would feel if she wasn't pregnant. He had taken some barroom punches that sent him to the hospital, but they were nothing compared to the blow her words had just delivered. Disappointment hit him hard, slicing deep.

Cade took a deep breath and released it slowly. Okay, it wasn't the end of the world, even if it did feel like it right now. He would go with plan B. And it would work. It had to.

BELLE WALKED ANGRILY out of Joseph Worthington's office. It was as she'd thought. She was caught between a rock and a hard place. The lawyer saw no way of removing Cade, short of a divorce, which of course she couldn't do. That meant living with him. What she had conceived as a perfect solution had backfired.

*Conceived.*

She didn't even want to think about Cade's suspicion that she might be pregnant. Of course, it was possible she wasn't. Her periods had never been regular. In fact, it wasn't unusual for her to go five or six weeks between periods or skip one altogether. So, there was probably nothing to worry about. If she didn't start by next week, then maybe it would be time to worry. Yeah. Next week.

Meanwhile, her main problem was waiting for her at home.

As she drove into the winery parking lot, Reese walked out to meet her.

"We may have a problem."

"Why am I not surprised. The line forms to the right. What's the matter?"

"I think we may have a price war on our hands. Several of the growers have called quoting some pretty high numbers from the other wineries."

"All of them?"

"No, just a few."

"I should have seen this coming."

"You got a crystal ball I don't know about?"

"Two weeks ago you mentioned the growers might ask for more. I knew you were right, but I let it slide."

"You've been distracted."

"I didn't take care of business, and they took advantage. Their timing is perfect. Harvest is just around the corner. Grandfather is gone. They're all waiting to see if I can cut it or not. What better time could they have?"

"Most of the growers are reasonable. Only a handful are pushing."

"Well, I'm not going to panic, but at the same time,

I can't afford to be nonchalant about the problem, either."

Reese removed his cowboy hat and swiped at the sweat on his brow with the sleeve of his shirt. "You'll handle it, Belle."

She smiled. "I appreciate the support. You know, I wonder if the rodeo circuit knows what a prize they lost the day you gave up the arena and came to work for my grandfather?"

Reese laughed. "Some decision. Ornery bulls with sharp horns or an ornery old man who probably forgot more about making wine than most vintners will ever know. Besides..." He resettled his hat on his head. "Rodeoing is a young man's sport. Or for a man who doesn't have anything to lose."

"Just the same, I'm grateful."

He tipped his hat. "Happy to oblige." Then he headed for the tasting room while Belle went to her office.

She spent the rest of the day working on plans for their participation in the Lone Star Wine Competition. Farentino was a small winery with a good reputation for quality, but winning awards would enhance their status. And it was happening. Perhaps a little too slowly for Belle's taste, but she reminded herself that wineries, like Rome, weren't built in a day. Llano Estacado, probably one of the largest operations in the area, certainly in the state, had been around since 1975 and was just starting to come into its own. Having only been established since the mid-eighties, Farentino was considered the new kid on the block. Every year their reputation grew, and next year their prized Estate Merlot would be ready. Belle had her heart set on first place in several competitions, which meant a lot of hard work.

She hadn't realized how much work until her grandfather had died. Even though she had worked alongside him, she'd never realized how much pressure came with making decisions until the mantle fell to her. Now, just when she should be feeling settled and ready to implement some of her marketing ideas, this thing with the growers had popped up. In her favor, she knew she was good with people, good at presenting her ideas clearly. If she could effectively put that gift to work in dealing with the growers, maybe a possible disaster could be averted.

LATE THE NEXT MORNING, her secretary buzzed her, announcing that Tom Carrington was on line two. Belle had hired Carrington a few weeks before to replace Cade as ranch foreman.

"Tom, what can I do for you?" Belle asked.

"It's McBride."

Wasn't it always? "What about him?"

"He came to me for a job. I told him no, figuring you didn't want him on the place. But then I decided maybe I spoke too quick, him being your husband and all."

"I see." There was no advantage to denying Cade a job. He would just find one elsewhere in the area, and he showed no intention of moving out. "Do we need to hire more help?"

"Well, actually, we do. It's time to bring the babies in off the range to be broke. Hard work, but Mc-Bride's qualified. I got to admit, he wouldn't be my first choice for a reliable hand with his reputation for hell-raisin', but I'll leave this one up to you."

"All right, go ahead. And Tom..."

"Yes, ma'am?"

"The ranch is your jurisdiction, and I trust your judgment. You could have handled this without a word to me, but I appreciate the fact that you called."

"Just doin' my job," Carrington said, and hung up.

Belle put the conversation out of her mind and focused on the problem worth her attention. She substituted lunch with a package of cheese crackers and a Coke, staying at her desk until her secretary poked her head in to say good-night. Weary and worried, she worked two more hours then drove home.

"Posey?" At this hour, the cook was usually gone, but as she opened the door it was obvious from the aroma coming from the kitchen that Posey was still there. Belle dropped her briefcase on the hall table, picked up the day's mail and sorted through it. "I hope you've got a lot of whatever I smell. I'm starved."

"I think we can accommodate you."

She glanced up to find Cade propped against the dining room doorway. "Oh...it's you." She hadn't forgotten about her "houseguest," she just hadn't expected him to be the greeting committee.

"Not the warmest welcome I ever got, but it'll do. Did I hear you mention you were hungry?"

"I went past hungry about three hours ago. I skipped lunch."

"How does chicken enchiladas with verde sauce followed by flan sound?"

Belle closed her eyes and sighed. "Like heaven."

"C'mon."

He headed toward the kitchen. "Posey left this for you in the warming oven." He slid a plate containing a generous helping of spicy Tex-Mex food in front of her as she sat down at the table.

While he poured himself a cup of coffee, she went to work on the enchiladas.

"Tough day?" he asked.

She spooned salsa onto a tortilla, rolled it up and took a bite. "Hmm."

"Is that a comment on the food or an answer to my question?"

"Both," she told him, reaching for another tortilla.

He poured her some coffee, then leaned against the edge of the counter and watched her while she ate, content to do just that. Watch her. There was something uncommonly soothing, almost intimate, about the two of them sharing a meal and coffee alone.

A few minutes later she sighed and pushed her plate away. "I think I'm going to live."

"That bad, huh?"

She rubbed the back of her neck. "You don't want to know."

Suddenly her hands were pushed away, replaced by his, massaging her neck. "Sure I do. Anything that can cause knots this big—" he kneaded her shoulder muscles "—must be trouble."

She was too tired to protest. Besides, his fingers were magic. "It looks like the grape growers are going to raise prices on us."

"You've always bought at a fair price."

Slowly, Belle began to relax under his talented fingers. "I know, but a few growers think it's time to push the price up. It's nothing new. In fact, traditionally, grape growers and wine makers have an adversarial relationship. Growers are paid by the ton, so naturally they want the largest crop possible. We want high quality, and sometimes that means a reduced crop level."

"But that's not the case here in the panhandle."

"Not until now."

"Why not?"

"In the beginning, we were the ones dealing with the issues like high sugar levels, low acidity." Her head lolled to one side as he worked his fingers up her neck then down between her shoulder blades. "Oh, that's fantastic."

"Right here?"

"Aa-a-h. What was I saying?"

"High sugar, low acid."

"Oh, yeah. Now the growers are more experienced. They solve some of our problems at the vine."

He finished the massage by gently rotating her shoulders. "So cooperate."

Belle's eyes popped open, and she twisted in her chair to face him. "Excuse me?"

"Find a way for the grape growers and wineries to share information and techniques. The more everyone knows, the better the crop, the better the wines."

"You mean like some kind of organization?"

"Whatever works."

The more she thought about his suggestion, the more she liked it. "That's...that's a wonderful idea, Cade. I had no idea you knew anything about wine making."

"I don't, but you couldn't hang around your grandfather for very long without learning something."

"It really is a marvelous idea. I'm going to talk to Reese first thing in the morning."

"Do yourself a favor. Let him run with it. He was born to organize. That's one of the reasons he was captain of the football team for three years."

"Oh, yes, the Fearsome Foursome."

Cade grinned. "I see our reputation has stood the test of time."

"Were you all really that bad?"

"Or good. Depending on who you asked."

"Girls, I'll wager."

"I'm not a 'kiss and tell' kinda guy."

"If you were, I'd be...uh, I mean, I didn't think you were...I just meant..."

Why didn't she just stick her size eights in her mouth and be done with it? "Uh, well—" she took her plate to the sink "—guess I better clean up after myself and get some sleep."

"Me, too."

Cade stretched, and out of the corner of her eye she couldn't help but admire his muscles. His entire body, in fact.

"Got broncs just waiting in line to be busted."

"Broncs? Oh, yes. Tom called me this morning to okay hiring you. I must say, he wasn't enthusiastic."

"Really." Cade wasn't surprised. The foreman had taken an instant dislike to him, and the feeling was mutual. He couldn't quite put his finger on the reason, but it had nothing to do with the fact that Carrington now held his former job. There was just something about the new foreman that didn't feel right, and Cade had relied on his instincts too long to ignore them. If Carrington wasn't on the up-and-up, he'd know it soon enough.

Cade shrugged. "Well, somebody's got to break 'em, and I need the work." He reached for her hand. "C'mon, I'll walk you upstairs."

It dawned on Belle that for the last few minutes, she had forgotten about their "marriage." She had been so comfortable in his presence, she'd forgotten to be coolly indifferent. When did this happen?

"Cade..."

"Yeah?"

They had reached her doorway, and for a heartbeat she thought about giving him his old job back, but her pride stopped her. Even if she did, Belle had a hunch his pride wouldn't let him accept. She shook her head. "Nothing. Never mind."

"Well, then...good night."

"Good—"

Before she knew what was happening, he caged her face in his hands and covered her mouth with his. The kiss was soft, tender and utterly delicious. Instinctively, she leaned against him, expecting him to take the kiss deeper. While her body yearned for precisely that, her mind tried to form the protest she knew she should voice.

But she never got the chance.

As quickly as it had begun, the kiss was over.

"Sweet dreams, darlin'." With that, he walked into his room and closed the door.

Belle stared after him. Why had he stopped? And why was she even asking? Her objective was to avoid his kisses, wasn't it? She needed to stay away from him in order to keep a cool head, didn't she? Well, she might achieve the cool head, but the rest of her was warm and resonating with need.

This was no good, she told herself as she touched a finger to her lips, still moist from his kiss. No good at all.

THE SOUND OF THE SHOWER running in Cade's bathroom woke her. She lay listening to the vibration through the walls, imagining him standing beneath the spray, soaping his chest, his powerful arms, his...

Belle groaned and pulled a pillow over her head. Not only was the man up before the sun, robbing her of sleep, but now he had her with her ear to the wall and her imagination running wild. "Back to sleep," she mumbled.

Then the shower stopped, and she found herself listening again. There was a short, silent pause, then more running water. She decided it was the sink this time. He must be shaving. And whistling? Could a man whistle and shave at the same time? Did he shave in the buff, or with just a towel wrapped around his waist?

There went her imagination again.

Belle yanked the pillow away, threw back the covers and went to her bathroom. If she couldn't stop eavesdropping, she might as well get ready and go to work. By the time she had showered, Cade was gone.

Dressed and ready for the office, she lingered in her grandfather's study, unnecessarily checking the scheduling pad. Truthfully, she had no real concerns regarding the ranch or its day-to-day operations. Tom Carrington was an adequate foreman, and the ranch was running smoothly, mostly thanks to the work Cade had done before he left. The bookkeeper kept her apprised with monthly reports. Truthfully, she didn't know why she was lingering. She actually spent very little time on the working part of the ranch, except for when a problem came up or when she went horseback riding.

Suddenly the idea of a ride sounded so inviting, she was tempted to indulge herself. But then she thought better of it. Was she really longing for the feeling of the wind on her cheeks? Or was riding away from responsibilities what truly tempted her? What difference did it make? She couldn't go dashing off on horseback, and that's all there was to it.

But the idea stayed with her through the day, and by midafternoon, she was too antsy to resist temptation. She drove home, changed into her jeans, boots and a T-shirt, grabbed a hat and headed straight for the barn. Most of the hands were still out, but she didn't mind saddling her own horse. In fact, it had been so long since she had done that, she was looking forward to it. As she passed the barn's side entrance, the one leading out to the round pen, she heard a familiar voice, every bit as hard to resist as her longing for a ride. As silently as possible, so as not to disturb Cade or his "pupil," she walked over to the railing of the round pen, hung her hat on a top post and watched.

Cade stood there with his back to her, working with one of the "babies," so called because they had spent all two years of their young lives in pastures. They'd never been touched, and had been brought straight off the range to be broken. The horse Cade was working with had already been wearing a halter and lead rope for two or three days, so he could step on the lead and get the connection between halter and rope. The step Cade was now beginning was referred to as "sack 'em out." The process consisted of desensitizing the horse using touch, smell and noise.

Belle was familiar with the breaking and training of the horses. Today her interest was in the trainer. Wearing jeans faded to white at the seams, an abused denim shirt with both sleeves missing, a damp, dust-caked bandanna around his neck and work gloves, he looked...dangerous. Men like Cade shouldn't be running around loose to wreak havoc on the female population. This particular population of one, at any rate.

As she watched, he took a burlap sack and began rubbing it over the horse's flank and buttocks, down the thigh of the back leg, over the hock right down to the fetlock, then up over the back, neck, shoulder and down the front leg. He covered every square inch of horseflesh. The animal stood still, except for an occasional quiver of muscles or a perking of his ears forward, demonstrating his alertness. The task completed, Cade discarded the burlap sack, then repeated the entire process using a plastic garbage bag. Again the horse's ears turned at the crackling of the plastic. Then Cade did the same thing again, only this time using a saddle pad. He saddled, then unsaddled, the horse, then saddled him again, careful not to pull the cinch too tight.

Belle was totally fascinated with the syncopation of movement and muscles. Both man and horse. As Cade worked, she saw the muscles of his back and of his powerful arms bunch and strain beneath his shirt. It was not a great leap for her to remember being held in those arms, remember the feeling of all his power directed at her, in her. No great stretch of imagination for her to recall the darkly passionate, obsessive need he had awakened in her. A need, despite all her efforts to ignore it, that was seldom far from her consciousness. Even now it simmered just below the surface of her control, threatening to overtake her, drive her back to that wildness she had tasted. And watching Cade, seeing his virility so well displayed, had definitely not helped. She was close to the boiling point; her body vibrated with sexual energy. She wanted him. If he turned and took her right here, right now, she would welcome it.

The realization streaked through her like lightning through a stormy sky, and she gasped, much as she had that first night when he caught her behind the knees, making her legs give way.

Cade heard her just as he was stepping up into the saddle. His head snapped up, and he missed the stirrup. For several seconds he simply stared at her from under the brim of his hat. Without breaking eye contact, he stopped his attentions to the horse and walked toward her with a lean-hipped saunter that had her heart beating faster.

"You're home early."

"I, uh, decided to take a ride."

He nodded. "How 'bout I get one of the boys to saddle Dolly for you?" he asked, referring to her favorite horse.

"Thanks, but I can do it." She hadn't moved, and he was now standing directly in front of her. And very close.

He yanked off his hat, wiped the sweat from his forehead, then crammed it back on his head. "Suit yourself."

She wished he would back up. It was hard to breathe with him so close. She tried to tell herself she was offended by the smell of healthy sweat on a hard male body, but her argument fell short of being convincing. "How many babies have you got?"

"Eighteen. Twelve colts and six fillies."

Somewhere in the back of her highly organized, detail-oriented mind was the thought that the number of horses should be higher. "Nice crop?" But her pulse was hammering so hard, she couldn't concentrate on anything but Cade's nearness.

"Seems to be." He couldn't take his eyes off the enticing pulse beat at the base of her throat, and he longed to taste that spot. "This one's got an attitude, but it won't last long."

Rather than meeting his gaze directly, she glanced away and took a step back. "Well, I guess I better go."

"Belle."

She stopped. "Yes?"

He reached over, nabbed her hat from the post and held it out to her. "Don't forget this. Wouldn't want any freckles across that pretty nose of yours."

"Thanks." She took the hat and walked back into the barn.

Cade watched her walk away, his hands clenched at his sides. He had almost fallen right on his ass when he heard that soft, surprised gasp. He flashed back to their one night together, and it had taken all his willpower not to cross the pen, rip her clothes off, throw her to the ground and take her. This testosterone hurricane that hit him every time he saw her wasn't going to cut it. How could he hope to win her heart if he got hard every time he got within ten feet of her?

Cade took a deep breath, then released it slowly. He had to get a grip on himself, and that was all there was to it. If he didn't, he would be certifiable by the end of the week.

He took several more deep breaths as he watched her walk through the barn. He wasn't crazy about the idea of her riding alone. Even though she knew the landscape well, there were dangers—rattlers, gopher holes—that could lead to trouble. He hadn't come this far to lose her to a skittish filly or diamondback. If she wasn't back in an hour, he was going after her.

BELLE KNEW SHE HAD PUSHED poor Dolly to the limit, racing her across the pasture. But she needed the speed, the rush, to take her mind off Cade. Not that she was completely successful. Damn him! Why couldn't he have stayed out of her life? Why couldn't he have just left well enough alone?

But had everything been "well" and "enough" after he left? Had she been happy? He wanted her, but he didn't love her, and that wasn't enough, so she'd sent him packing. Had that satisfied her? The fact of the matter was, she was as miserable without him as she professed to be with him.

So here she was again, caught between that ever present rock and that damned hard place. Stuck, and by her own design.

While she mused, she had slowed Dolly to a walk without even realizing it. The filly snorted, tossing her head. Belle reached down and patted her neck.

"Sorry, sweetie. I was taking out my aggression on you."

She kicked Dolly into an easy lope along the bed of dry ravine, up a grassy rise, then abruptly reined her in.

There was a rider approaching, and the instant she saw him, Belle knew exactly who it was. Why couldn't he just leave her alone?

# 6

FOR A HEARTBEAT Belle thought about turning around and riding away as fast as she could, but she didn't. He would just come after her. In a few minutes, Cade reined his bay to a halt beside her.

"It's getting late. Maybe you better head in."

"What are you, my nanny? I'm a big girl, Cade. I can ride my little pony all by myself. And this is August. The sun won't be down for another three hours. I know this range as well as you do, and if I had wanted company I would have asked for it."

His only response was to glare at her.

"In case that went over your head...*get...lost.*" She kicked Dolly's flank and trotted off.

Well, that was just great. He'd been worried half out of his mind, and *she* was the one throwing a tantrum. He spurred the bay and quickly caught up with her. Moving so fast his hand was only a blur, he jerked Dolly's reins free, then kicked his horse into a gallop.

Startled, Belle could only grab for the saddle horn and hang on for dear life.

The bay skidded to a stop at a stand of live oaks, and Cade jerked Dolly to a halt and dismounted.

"Get down."

Even if he'd had a neon sign hanging over his head flashing Danger, Danger, she was too furious to heed the warning.

"Have you lost your mind?"

"Probably. Now, get down off that horse before I take you down."

"No."

"You're acting like a brat."

"Me? What do you think you're doing, yanking those reins out of my—"

Cade hauled her out of the saddle and literally carried her into the shade of the largest tree. His mouth took possession of hers before her feet ever touched the ground. He knew he should temper the kiss, in fact, stop altogether, but he couldn't. A rush of possessiveness flooded his senses, distorted his perspective, and he *had* to touch her. For Cade, the sensation was unexpected, and definitely unwanted. And it got all tangled up with his intellect, creating a snarl of emotions that put him on unfamiliar ground. While part of him called out for sanity, another part told him to stake his claim on this woman who had him twisting in the wind and didn't even know it. What was this power she had that made him lose all control?

Reason demanded she stay in control, stay distant. But she couldn't help being pulled into the kiss as if she were being pulled into a maelstrom. She had to fight it, to save herself. Belle dug the heels of her hands into his shoulders and pushed him away. "Don't," she warned.

"Stop fighting me, Belle."

"Stop pushing me." She backed up into Dolly and could go no farther.

"Pushing? Hell, I'd have to catch you first." He stepped closer. Yanking off his gloves, he slid one hand to the back of her neck and pulled her against him. "Come to think of it, looks like that's what I've done."

This time his kiss was harder, deeper, and he seemed hell-bent on overriding any resistance. She struggled to keep her mind free even as her body surrendered, but it was useless. What was this power he had over her? Why couldn't she break free and stay that way? But she was helpless against the hunger he created. The hunger that only he could satisfy.

"Don't do this...." She wanted to devour his mouth even as she begged him to stop. "Please, Cade."

"I can't let you keep running."

"Why?"

"Because there's you, and there's me. And then there's what we are together. And it's good, Belle. Better than good. Can you look me in the eye and honestly tell me you don't want that? Don't want me?"

Want. He wanted her and she wanted him. That

was all he saw, all he would accept. All she could expect.

"No," she whispered, disappointed in her lack of conviction. "I want you. There. Satisfied? You've made me admit I'm a human being with needs. Are you happy now?"

God, the pain in her eyes was like a knife to his heart. He could kick himself for coming after her, trying to force her to see what he was so certain was the truth. But when she hadn't returned from her ride, he'd begun to imagine all sorts of hellish scenarios. All of them involved Belle, lying somewhere hurt and bleeding. Even now, with her safe in his arms, his stomach rolled just thinking about his fears.

He removed his hands and stepped away. "I'm sorry, Belle. I had no right to do that."

She turned, crammed her foot into the stirrup and stepped up on Dolly. "I'm going back."

He let her go. Not because he wanted to, but because he knew he had just made a big mistake. He couldn't force Belle to love him, no matter how badly he wanted it. If he did, he would crush her spirit, one of the things he loved most about her. Worse, he would wound her pride. And he was at least smart enough to realize that if he did that, she would never forgive him.

No, today was a big mistake. Just when he thought he had taken two steps forward in his master plan, he was knocked back a step. He mounted and rode back to the ranch, careful to keep his distance.

By the time he returned, groomed his horse, took a shower and came down for dinner, she had taken a tray of food and gone upstairs. Obviously, she had no desire for his company.

Okay, he thought. He had to find some way to make up for lost time. And it better be good.

Stretched out on the bed, her sable brown hair still damp from her shower, Belle stared at the ceiling, thinking about her humiliation.

"I will not cry." She punched her doubled-up fist into the down comforter. "That's one satisfaction he'll have to live without."

A cramp, small but annoying, knotted her stomach. She hadn't eaten since lunch, and was now ignoring the food on the tray she had made for herself. That was probably it. Her stomach was growling....

But what if it wasn't?

Until that moment she had forgotten about the chance she might be pregnant. What if her ride had done something, caused something to go wrong?

The thought was too terrifying, too heartbreaking to comprehend.

How could she have been so careless? If she was carrying Cade's child, all of this tension couldn't be doing him any good. *Him*. Why did she assume the baby would be a him? *If*, and it was still a big if, there even was a baby. She had no symptoms that she was aware of. And she hadn't noticed any physical changes. Would there be any in only six weeks? Morning sickness? Light-headedness? Belle felt as if she were asking these questions about someone else.

Of course, she'd dreamed of becoming a mother someday. Of finding a man who would love her, and be a strong, loving father to her children, but it had always just been a dream. A distant future.

Now it might soon be a reality.

Tomorrow, she decided, she would buy one of those home pregnancy kits and find out. If she wasn't pregnant, then she could relax. And if she was...?

Well, it was better to know the truth. No matter how complicated it made her already entangled life, at least she would know for sure and be able to deal with the consequences.

Belle waited for another cramp, and when it didn't come, she whispered a sigh of relief. Instinctively, she rolled onto her side, cradling her tummy with her arm, her grandmother's prediction echoing in her mind.

Pride might very well be her undoing.

"MORNIN'."

The last person Cade expected to find waiting in the kitchen was Reese. "Good morning. Where's Belle?"

"Left about ten minutes ago. Said she had an errand to run, but she'd be back within a half hour."

Cade propped his hands on his hips. "Damn."

"Want me to give her a message?"

The kind of message he wanted delivered had to be done face-to-face. Apologies were hard enough. He doubted Belle would take kindly to one relayed through a third party.

"No, thanks."

Reese shrugged and poured himself another cup of coffee.

"Why aren't you at the winery?" Cade asked.

"I'm waiting for Belle. We've got a meeting—the first meeting—of the High Plains Growers Association. Belle told me about your suggestion. It's a beaut."

"That's all it was, a suggestion. You and Belle are making it happen."

"Not me—Belle. Most of the growers, and a couple of the wine makers, are due here in about twenty minutes to discuss establishing an organization to share information and technology. It's just a preliminary meeting, but we've contacted all the growers in the area, and they're behind it one hundred percent."

"Why meet here? Why not at the winery?"

Reese downed the last of his coffee. "Belle thought the growers might feel more comfortable. Less inhibited. She wants them to feel that this is as much their organization as it is the vintners', right from the start. This is going to end any more talk of a price war.

That's some woman you're married to, ace. Even if you're only pretending."

"Who says I'm pretending?" The words were out before he realized what he was saying.

"Excuse me?"

"Nothing." Great. Now he'd done it.

"Oh, no, you don't get off that easy. Aren't you the man who told me this marriage was just for looks? Business, and nothing more."

"Yeah."

"Well?"

"Well, what?"

"You gonna tell me what's going on, or do I have to drag it out of you?"

"I'm...I love her, okay?"

"Well, I'll be damned."

"That's exactly what Logan said. And if I want that broadcasted, I'll call the radio station, you got it?"

"Yeah, I got it. Since Logan thinks marriage is for idiots, I suppose he said you were A, crazy for coming back, and B, brainless for coming back to a woman who only wanted a hired husband."

"Words to that effect."

"How does she feel about this?"

"Beats the hell out of me."

"Whoa. You mean you haven't told her?"

Cade glanced away. "I've been busy."

Chuckling, Reese shook his head. "Busy, huh."

Then he couldn't hold back, and the chuckle rolled into a deep laugh.

"What's so damned funny?"

"You. Her. I've never seen two more stubborn, pig-headed people in my life. You two deserve each other."

"After yesterday, I'm sure Belle wouldn't agree with you."

Reese's laughter faded. "You haven't done anything massively stupid, have you?"

"Define *massive*."

"Like the time you tried to make Wanda Lange jealous and wound up without a date to the senior prom?"

"Close."

"I suppose you want Belle to come to you."

"Sure would make things easier, but I'm not holding my breath."

Reese set his empty cup down, folded his arms across his chest and gave Cade a hard look. "You're the best friend I've got, but friendship or not, I wouldn't like to see Belle hurt."

Cade recognized a warning when he heard one, but then, Reese always did fancy himself a knight in shining armor. "Don't get your nose outta joint. I have no intention of hurting her."

"Mighty glad to hear it. What *are* you going to do?"

"Apologize for my stupidity, to begin with."

"Now, there's a sight I'd buy a ticket to see. Cade

McBride, Casanova of the caprock, groveling before a woman who'll probably spit in his eye."

"She's definitely not an easy sell." Cade smiled. "But worth the effort."

"Good luck, ace. My money's on you." Reese slapped him on the shoulder. "Bustin' broncs is probably easier."

The mention of broncs reminded Cade of something that had been bothering him since yesterday. "Speaking of broncs, how many babies do you think we should have? I know you haven't been involved with the day-to-day operations in over a year, but take a guess."

"Twenty, twenty-five."

"Eighteen." At Reese's dubious expression, Cade added, "I personally counted twenty-two in the spring, all branded. You haven't sold any in the last few weeks, have you?"

"Not that I'm aware of."

"What do you know about Carrington?"

"Not much. Worked for a stock contractor by the name of John Tanner up in Borger. He knows his stuff. Why?"

"Just curious. Heard about anybody missing any stock lately? Horses or cattle?"

"Just curious, my butt. You think Carrington is rustling stock, don't you?"

"I didn't say that."

"You implied it. Granted, it wouldn't be the first

time an employee was behind missing stock, but that's no reason to set up a vigilante committee and go lookin' for a rope. And to answer your question, no, I haven't heard of anyone losing any stock."

"If you hear anything, let me know. And don't mention any of this to Belle, all right?"

"Fat chance, since I think you've lost your marbles, anyway."

"Don't mention 'what' to Belle?"

Cade and Reese turned to find her standing in the kitchen doorway.

"That I think your new foreman isn't much on organization. He's letting some things slide around here," Cade said with a warning glance at Reese.

"And I suppose you think you could do better."

"No supposing to it, darlin'."

"Well, too bad. I own the winery *and* this ranch, and I personally hired Tom. He had excellent references, and he's done a wonderful job so far. You left your position, Cade. Did you really expect to find it waiting for you?"

The implication went far beyond the job of ranch foreman, and they both knew it.

Belle turned and left the room. Reese gave his friend a you-asked-for-it shrug and followed her.

Damn, Cade thought. If what he suspected was true, she wasn't going to take kindly to the fact that she'd made a mistake in hiring Carrington. For that reason alone, he had to make certain he could prove his suspicions. And the quicker, the better. He still owed Belle an apology, but that was personal. Now he owed her his loyalty, and he'd start by making sure she wasn't being ripped off.

Her heart was in the winery, and it always would be. But that didn't mean she could neglect the ranch. Of course, up until recently, he had been there to ensure there were no glitches, leaving her free to tend to the winery. Both operations were independent, profitable and demanding. But one person couldn't run both. It had to do with time, not skill or gender. But Belle thought she could handle both. God knew her pride wouldn't allow her to think anything else. And as if she didn't have enough on her plate, he was beginning to worry that she had skipped grieving for Caesar and thrown herself into her work. She never spoke of him, remembered him. It was as if she had pushed his passing, and all that it meant, to the back of her mind. That might be all right for a while, but sooner or later she would have to deal with the grief, and it would probably hit her when she least expected it.

He couldn't face that for her, but he could help. He could, and would, handle the other situation by simply sidestepping her pride and doing this on his own. And if Carrington was dipping his pen in company ink, then he would have to find a way to let Belle think she was handling that, as well.

From the study, Belle heard the front door close as

Cade left. Conversations were crisscrossing between growers, but she was having difficulty concentrating. Partly because she was irritated that Cade had the nerve to think Tom wasn't an adequate replacement, but mostly because she kept thinking about the items she had purchased on her errand before the meeting.

A pregnancy test. Two, in fact. One for a backup in case the first one failed.

They were innocuous-looking packages, but within them was the possibility of a life-changing result. She wanted to dash upstairs right now and conduct the test, but she couldn't. And she had a full calendar until four o'clock. There was no way she could sneak back here, and she didn't dare do the test at work. No, she needed privacy. She would have to wait.

But it was going to be a long day.

IT WAS BLUE.

Belle didn't want to believe it, but there it was, proof positive. She stared at the tester, trying desperately to tell herself it was a mistake. But in her heart, she knew the truth. To be certain, she would repeat the test, but it was just a formality.

She was pregnant with Cade's baby.

Sitting at her vanity behind the locked door of her bathroom, she couldn't take her eyes off the square of blue that had changed her future. No, that wasn't true. She had done that the minute she asked Cade to marry her.

The blue blurred as tears filled her eyes. She had never felt so alone in her life. So displaced, and alone.

Without even realizing her destination, she went downstairs, instinctively seeking the sanctuary of her grandfather's study.

She didn't turn on the light, preferring the solitude of the approaching darkness. Stepping across the threshold, she paused, inundated with the smells and textures of the room, with her grandfather's presence. A tidal wave of memories rolled over her, and suddenly all her frustration over the will, her rage at his lack of trust, was unmasked. Unmasked, and condensed into one staggeringly painful truth.

She wasn't angry and hurt because of some legal document.

With tears streaming down her face, Belle's hands doubled into fists at her side. She was furious because he'd left her. The last person who loved her was gone.

And she missed him. Desperately.

Her heart broke with the longing just to see him one more time. To hear his voice. She wanted to sit in this room and tell him everything, the good and the bad. And have him listen. No matter what, he always listened. He was her family, and now she had only distant connections to people she had never met. The shock, the total alienation, hit her like a slap in the face.

Then all of the fight drained out of her.

All the driving need to preserve her pride, to protect her heart at all costs, flowed out of her like some evil spirit finally departing. Her knees threatened to give way.

Between darkness and tears, she relied on touch rather than sight to guide her to his tasting chair, sliding onto the cushions as if being hugged by an old friend.

Her grandfather. Oh, God, how she missed him. Missed their spirited debates that occasionally turned into arguments. His unnerving habit of jumping from English into his still-fluent Italian whenever she made a point he didn't want to acknowledge. But most of all, she missed his strength. No matter what happened between them, she had always known she could depend on that strength. Now she was alone.

No. Resting her head against the backrest, she touched her still-flat stomach. She wasn't completely alone.

CADE FOUND HER in the study.

"Belle?"

When she didn't answer, alarm bells sounded in his head. He went down on one knee beside the chair and picked up her hand. It was limp and icy cold. "Darlin', are you all right?"

"You can—can still smell his pipe tobacco in here," she whispered. "I—I loved that blend he always smoked. Sort of sweet, woodsy."

Cade let out a breath he hadn't even realized he'd

been holding. As he had predicted, grief had smacked her right between the eyes, and she was sitting in the dark crying her guts out. "I know, darlin', but I think you—"

"He was reading that book the day he... I can't close it."

Cade looked around. Even in the growing darkness, he realized that the room was exactly as it had been the day he and Belle had struck their marriage deal. Exactly as it had always looked.

She hadn't changed a thing.

Bits of memory popped into his consciousness. Of Belle smoothing her fingertips over her grandfather's worn scheduling pad, despite the anger in her voice. Of her yelling at him not to touch anything.

She hadn't changed one single thing. Not a piece of paper on the desk. Not a book on the shelf. Not even the one window with the blinds pulled halfway up. If possible, Caesar Farentino could walk back into this room in the next second and find it precisely as he had left it.

When Cade looked back at Belle, the expression on her face made his heart stop. Tears, rivers of them, coursed down her cheeks, but she didn't even notice. She stared straight ahead.

"They went away and left me."

Oh, God.

"All of them. He promised he wouldn't, but..."

"C'mon, baby. You can't stay in here."

"He's so close when I'm in this room."

"Belle—"

"I have to stay here. That's what I need to do. What if he comes back and I'm not here?"

He wasn't going to be able to talk her out of this, and he was afraid to remove her against her will. No telling what that might do to her. "All right, but I'm not leaving you alone."

She turned her head as if hearing his voice for the first time. "You won't—you won't leave me alone?"

"No, darlin', I won't."

"Promise?"

It was a child's plea, and it ripped his heart out. "I promise."

"That's nice."

Her tears had stopped, but she was so lethargic she scared him. Her mind was trying to cope, but she was dazed with all the fresh grief.

He stood up, then gently lifted her in his arms and sat down in the chair, cradling her. She snuggled into the curve of his neck like a trusting child, and sighed. "Nice," she whispered.

Cade held her until her deep, even breathing told him she was asleep. Then he rose and carried her upstairs. He paused in front of her door for only a second before making his decision. No separate rooms tonight. It might not be the way he had envisioned it, but it didn't matter. Tonight Mr. and Mrs. Cade McBride would share the same bed.

He settled her beneath the covers, then stretched out on top beside her, carefully lifting her head to rest on his shoulder. Again she snuggled against him as if it were the most natural thing in the world. It sure felt natural.

As he lay with her in his arms, Cade thought about how she might feel tomorrow. He could have a familiar hellcat on his hands, bound and determined to hang on to her pride, or he could wake up with...hope.

# 7

BELLE YAWNED, turned over in bed and rolled right up against... What was that?

Slowly she opened her eyes. "Cade?"

"You feeling better, darlin'?"

"Better?" Everything was slightly out of focus, as though she were waking up after a night of drinking, and not enough good sense. "Was I sick?" She glanced down, then around. "Where am..." Her head snapped up. "This is your room."

"Uh-huh."

She was on the verge of blasting him with accusations of kidnapping, and Lord knew what else, when she remembered last night. She started to cry. "I—I—"

"It's okay."

She sniffed, swiping at the tears. "I don't remember coming upstairs."

He leaned over to the table near his side of the bed, yanked a tissue from a box and handed it to her. "Maybe because you were asleep at the time. I carried you."

In the process of drying her face, Belle stopped. "Why didn't you put me in my own room?"

He stared at her for several seconds. "You needed me."

His words brought everything back with startling clarity. The grief overwhelming her to the point of obliterating all else. And Cade. Talking so sweetly...

"Grandfather's study." She inhaled deeply, then released the breath slowly. "I thought I had dealt with his death, but last night all this...emotion came out of nowhere and...sort of blindsided me."

"That's what I figured."

"I've been so angry, Cade, and I didn't know why."

He brushed a wisp of hair back from her cheek. "You were like a cork under pressure, darlin'. Sooner or later you were going to pop."

"And you had to clean up the mess."

"I didn't mind."

Dry-eyed, she looked at him. "Thank you."

"You're welcome."

He wanted to pull her into his arms and just hold her, but he wasn't sure she would allow it. True, she seemed to have mellowed, but that didn't mean she was ready for the kind of changes he wanted in their relationship. Particularly after this new round of grief.

"Well," Belle said, feeling more awkward by the minute. She slipped out of bed, intending to make a quick retreat, but a wave of dizziness hit her. She swayed.

Cade was out of bed and had her in his arms in a heartbeat. "You okay?"

"I—I think I stood up too fast. Or maybe it's just because I skipped dinner last night."

"You're making a habit of skipping meals, and it's coming to a halt as of today."

Grateful for his support, she lingered in his arms for a moment or two longer than she needed to. He was so strong, it was hard to resist leaning on him, physically and emotionally. And he was being so nice to her. She looked up at him. "Yes, sir."

It took every ounce of willpower Cade had not to kiss her. They had taken a couple of major steps, he reminded himself. Don't blow it for a quick taste of her mouth. But it was such a tempting mouth. Such a soft, full—

"I think I'm steady on my feet now."

"What? Oh, yeah. But I want you to go downstairs and let Posey fix you a big breakfast." He fully expected her to protest his arrogant attitude, so he decided he might as well go the whole way. "And then I want you to eat every—"

"If you'll join me."

"Join you? Uh, sure."

"I'll shower and be down in about twenty minutes, okay?"

"Deal."

Well, this was a twist. Now what? he wondered. Then decided, who cares? At least she wasn't giving him the cold shoulder. She had invited him to join her for breakfast, and he wasn't going to look a gift horse in the mouth.

Cade was waiting for her when she got downstairs, propped against the counter, one boot crossed over the other. He must have showered, too, and fast, because his hair was still wet. Dark blond strands curled over his shirt collar, leaving the cotton damp. She had never noticed that his hair was so wavy, or maybe it was only when it was wet. Wet or dry, he was still one of the best-looking men she had ever seen.

She looked good enough to eat. All fresh and sweet-smelling. Cade's mouth watered just looking at her. Last night had been a little bit of heaven and hell for him. The chance to hold her was bliss, but he knew that it might be his only chance if he didn't play his cards right. He still couldn't afford to rush, even if she was smiling at him so sweetly.

"Cade?"

"Uh, you...want some scrambled eggs? Bacon?" He reached for two plates.

"No." The thought of even a drop of grease made her stomach roil. Oh, no, she couldn't get sick in front of him. When she looked up to find him scowling at her, she quickly added, "No, thanks. I think I'll have a bran muffin and some yogurt."

He wrinkled his nose. "Sissy food. Are you on some kind of diet?"

"No, do I...do you think I need to be?" Had she gained weight? Her mirror told her no, but maybe he saw something she didn't.

"I think you're perfect just the way you are."

His compliment flowed through her like warm honey, sweet and golden. "Th-thanks." And I could say the same about you, she wanted to add.

He spooned a generous helping of eggs onto his plate. "My stomach just can't get excited about a bunch of whole grains and live cultures."

"I'll have to work on you."

He stepped close, handing her a plate. "I'm all yours."

"I'll...I'll remember that."

After a couple of seconds staring at her mouth, Cade forced himself to move away from her. He sat down at the table and concentrated on lifting his fork to his mouth. And it took effort.

When she joined him, instead of taking the chair on the opposite side of the table, she pulled out the one next to him and sat down. He took it as a good sign. Definitely encouraging. Enough to give him the courage to take the next step in his plan.

"You got a full day?"

"Not really."

His luck was holding. "I was thinking about maybe taking in a movie. Interested?"

Belle blinked. "A movie?"

"And afterward—if you're hungry, of course—we could get a bite to eat."

"Are you...asking me out? I mean like on a... date?" Given their unusual situation, the idea sounded bizarre but sweet.

"More or less."

"Which is it? More, or less?"

"More."

She smiled, feeling better than she had in...well, she couldn't even remember when. "I'd love to go with you."

"Good. Great. I'll, uh, check to see when the feature starts and call you."

"Wonderful." Still smiling, she left the table, her meal barely touched.

Cade was so thrilled he didn't even notice. It was a start.

But it might get stopped cold when she found out what he had learned about Tom Carrington, Cade reminded himself.

He had called Carrington's former employer yesterday, and discovered the foreman hadn't received quite the glowing praise his letter of reference had stated. In fact, according to John Tanner, Carrington had been fired.

For suspicion of theft.

Some valuable rodeo stock had turned up missing, and Carrington had been in the right place at the right time. They were never able to prove he was responsible, but Tanner was convinced enough to let him go.

But how was he going to let Belle know without destroying this fragile new truce of theirs?

RUBYDELL BOOKBINDER looked up as Reese and Cade walked into the Sweetwater Springs Café. "Well, ain't you two bright and early."

"And starvin'," Cade said. "How about some of your pancakes and a big slice of ham?"

"You got it, sugar. Coffee?"

Cade glanced around until he found the men he expected to find and gave Reese a sly nudge. "Yeah. And keep it comin'," he told her as he strolled over to where the boys were sitting.

"Hey, Reese. Cade." Smitty grinned.

"Mornin', boys. Mind if we join you?"

Old Walt elbowed Alvin to scoot over. "Pull up a chair."

"Rubydell," Cade called over his shoulder. "Put the boys' coffee on my tab."

"Thanks, Cade."

"Yeah, thanks."

"No problem."

Cade knew that if he maneuvered the three in the right direction, they were better at reporting the news than the *Sweetwater Springs Gazette*. The trick was making it look like it was their idea to talk, not him pumping them for information.

"What you fellas doin' in town?" Alvin asked.

"Reese had to stop by the feed store, and I'm just along for the ride," Cade informed them. "We're running low, and our regular order won't be delivered till the end of the week. Right, Reese?"

"Yeah. I swear, feed disappears so fast. If I didn't know better, I'd think somebody was taking it."

"That guy from Arkansas who bought the Freelander place came into the feed store saying how his trailer and a bunch of feed came up missin'," Smitty announced.

Alvin shot him an annoyed look. "You didn't tell us that."

"Don't tell you everythin' I know."

Old Walt grunted. "Since when?"

"Trailers and feed go missin' more often than not," Alvin said.

"Makes up nearly seventy-five percent of all the ranch thievin' in the state. And that's a fact," Old Walt pointed out.

Rubydell served the food and Cade quickly cut a bit of ham. "I've got no use for thieves."

The other three sipped their coffees and nodded their agreement.

"Well, now." Old Walt rubbed his stubbled chin as Rubydell served Reese his breakfast. "I'm not one to gossip, and that's a fact." The waitress rolled her eyes and poured more coffee all around. "But you got to figure every rumor has a grain of truth to it."

"You gonna tell them 'bout Cotton Johnson?" Smitty wanted to know.

"Yeah. Works over at the Rockin' H," Alvin added.

"Well," Walt continued, "he was in here three days ago complainin' about how the count on their two-year-olds was down, and how the foreman was chewin' on his butt for messin' up the count."

Reese slathered butter over his pancakes and drowned them in syrup. "You don't say."

"I do. And Cotton told me he counted them babies in the spring, and he knew damned well a couple of 'em was gone."

"This is the first I've heard about it," Reese said.

"Happened in the last four to six weeks, but you're stuck out there makin' wine, so I ain't surprised you didn't know."

"They report it to the sheriff?" Cade asked.

"Beats me. Cotton said it weren't no skin off his nose 'long as the foreman got off his back about it."

Alvin turned to Reese. "Farentino spread missin' any stock?"

"Nope. Every head accounted for," he lied.

Alvin gestured to Rubydell for a refill. "That's good." The others nodded agreement.

"Say, what you been up to, Cade? Ain't hardly seen much of you since you come home." Smitty smiled his toothless grin, while Walt leaned in, anxious for any tidbit of gossip.

"Just keeping busy." Cade decided they had gotten

all they were going to get from these three. He pushed his plate away, wiped his mouth with his napkin and reached for his coffee. Over the rim, he gave Reese a look that indicated he was ready to leave.

"Well, I'd like nothing better than to sit and jaw with you boys all day, but I got work to do." Reese downed the coffee and stood up.

"See ya, Reese."

"Yeah, thanks for the coffee."

"Anytime." Reese walked to the cash register, paid his bill, gave the men a short wave and left.

"That Reese Barrett is a nice fella," Alvin observed.

Old Walt leaned back in his chair. "Yeah, but he don't talk much."

"ALL RIGHT," REESE SAID as he and Cade drove back to the ranch. "Go ahead and say, 'I told you so.'"

"Now, what kind of friend would I be to do a thing like that?"

"Yeah, right. So what do we do, ace?"

"We?"

"Whatever scheme you've hatched probably takes at least two men. I owe you, anyway, for doubting you about Carrington. You need backup. You got it. So long as we don't break any laws."

"Actually, all I need is for you to do your job."

Reese frowned. "I don't get it."

"You will."

A DATE. CADE HAD ASKED her out on a date. She still couldn't believe it. This time yesterday, she would have bet money that they'd end up killing each other, not dating. But then, this time yesterday, she hadn't faced a reality she had been avoiding for more than two months.

For the first time since her grandfather's funeral, she could admit to her oppressive loneliness. To the grief that constantly threatened tears. Had she cried at the funeral? She couldn't remember. That fact alone was telling. Was it any wonder anger had consumed her? Beneath it lay raw fear. How could she face that? The anger was much easier to deal with. Anger at her grandfather for leaving her, and then more anger, because of his will. Anger at Cade for disrupting her well-organized plan. And anger at herself for her brief lapse in controlling her passions the night she married Cade.

Looking back, Belle wondered, if she hadn't unleashed her rage over that silly wedding bouquet, would she have found some other way to punish herself? Probably. Her feelings of abandonment had deep roots. Caesar's death was the final blow, the final abandonment, and anger was her only coping mechanism. It seemed so simple, so obvious, but, of course, she had been deaf, dumb and blind to all of that until a tall, sexy cowboy had awakened feelings and longings she'd been suppressing for years.

The intercom buzzed, and her secretary announced

that her doctor's office was on the line. Belle had called for an appointment the moment she got to work.

"Isabella Farent—uh, McBride," she answered.

"This is Dr. Jordan's receptionist. Two of the doctor's OB patients have gone into labor, and I'm afraid we will have to reschedule your appointment."

Belle's spirit sank. She wanted to confirm her pregnancy as soon as possible. "I was hoping to see him today."

"Well, let me see." Pause. "This is his night at the clinic. He could see you there around six-thirty. Will that do?"

It meant canceling her date. She was torn. She wanted to be with Cade, wanted to see if they had a chance to make their make-believe marriage real. But realistically, what chance would she have when he found out about the baby? Who was she kidding?

No one but herself.

"That will be fine," she told the receptionist. Then she hung up.

Belle stared at the phone, dreading the next call. Finally, she picked up the receiver, dialed the ranch and left a message for Cade to call her.

She tried to concentrate on a sample contract she was preparing to submit to the new growers association, but she kept glancing at the phone. Finally, she gave up and went to the tasting room to look in on the tasting of the Estate Merlot. But even then, she kept waiting for her secretary to page her. Another hour crawled by before he called.

"What's up?"

"I...Cade, I'm sorry, but I have to cancel our date."

There was a long silence on the other end of the line.

"Cade?"

"What made you change your mind?"

"Nothing! I wanted...I want to be with you tonight, but something has come up that I have to deal with."

"Can't you postpone it until tomorrow?"

"Believe me, I wish I could. But I can't."

"Belle, are you okay?"

"Of course, why wouldn't I be?" she asked, suddenly nervous. He couldn't suspect anything.

"You sound tired."

"Yes," she said, relieved. "Yes, I am." Pause. "But not too tired to ask for a rain check on the movie."

"Anytime."

"I'm going to hold you to that."

"Fine by me."

"Thanks for being so understanding."

"Yeah, that's me all over."

Belle had to smile. "See you later." And she hung up.

BY THE TIME SIX-THIRTY rolled around, saying she was tired was no longer a lie. Belle was exhausted. Thankfully, the doctor was able to see her on time. He ran blood and urine tests, listened to her heart and took some general health and family history information since it had been well over a year since she'd had a checkup. In no time at all he had the results and gave her a stack of pamphlets to read and a copy of the lab report confirming beyond a doubt that she was pregnant. About six weeks along, he told her, allowing a few days on either side for the day of conception.

She could have told him the exact day of conception, Belle thought, driving home. The exact hour, in fact. And the thought that someday she would have to confess to her child that he, or she, had been conceived in a sleeping bag at a Boy Scout camp lacked a certain appeal.

Her child. And Cade's.

For the first time, Belle realized that she wanted this child more than she had ever dreamed.

Because it was Cade's baby.

And because she was in love with Cade.

Oh, Lord, she thought. It was true. Worse, she had been in love with him from the moment he had first kissed her. For an instant she tried to tell herself she only *thought* she loved him because it was a substitute for her recent loss.

But that idea had about as much strength as wet tissue paper. The fact was, she had loved and wanted Cade McBride long before her grandfather died.

The question was, what should she do about it?

She had depended on her pride as a shield for so

long, she wasn't sure she could step out from behind it. Wasn't sure she could risk that kind of vulnerability. Not where Cade was concerned. And yet, taking the risk was the only way she would ever have what she truly wanted.

Of course, she still had to tell him about the baby. It wasn't going to be easy, but she had no control over how he would take the news.

*No control.*

For the first time in her life, Belle had to admit that not being in control had a positive side.

Along with that came the admission that it had been unfair of her to offer Cade the husband-for-hire deal in the first place. She'd taken advantage of him, and she felt guilty about it. She had waved a big fat deed under his nose, more than he could have gotten on his own. The only fair thing to do was let him off the hook, which, of course, she couldn't do.

Belle braked the Suburban to a stop in front of the house and reached to unfasten her seat belt. It refused to budge until the third try and she made a mental note to have it fixed. She flipped open her briefcase. She put the lab report and pamphlets inside to keep them from curious eyes, then closed the case and got out. The steps were an effort, and her feet felt as if they had lead weights strapped to her ankles. If she could scrape up enough energy to make it upstairs, she could collapse on the bed. She reached for the doorknob, and the door flew open.

"Hey there, darlin'."

"Cade." Just the sight of him lifted her spirits, and when he smiled at her, she could almost forget her weariness. "I didn't expect you to wait around—"

He leaned close as she stepped inside. "Did you think I'd go without you?"

"Well, I...you work hard—"

"No harder than you do."

"And you have so little free time—"

"That's why I choose to spend it carefully."

"You should have gone without—"

"We had a date, remember."

"I know, but—"

"No buts." He took her briefcase. "Anyway, you look beat. Probably the last thing you want to do is go out."

Ironically, she had felt totally drained until she opened the door and found him waiting for her. Now everything seemed less heavy, lighter.

"Why don't you go upstairs and change into something comfortable? I've got a surprise for you."

"You've...got a surprise for me?" She couldn't remember the last time anyone had surprised her. "What is it?"

"Oh, no you don't. Go change."

"But—"

"You heard me." He pointed toward the staircase. "Get."

"I'm going, I'm going. But under protest—"

"Now, there's a shock."

"Teasing someone about a surprise is cruel."

"Would you prefer I carried you upstairs and undressed you myself?"

Belle's mouth fell open, but she quickly recovered. "Give me five minutes."

"You've got ten."

In her bedroom, she threw off her work clothes and grabbed her jeans. But when she zipped them, they felt a little tight. But how could that be? She had worn those jeans yesterday and they'd fit just fine. Come to think of it, they had been snug, but she'd dismissed it because they were new and not yet washed to a soft, comfortable fit. And yesterday she hadn't known for sure that she was pregnant. Maybe her mind was playing tricks on her. Still, what if wearing tight clothes wasn't good for the baby? Soon she wouldn't be able to fit into the jeans at all.

Belle stepped out of the jeans and tossed them onto her bed. Then, wearing nothing but her bikini panties and bra, she walked over to her full-length mirror.

Her eyes beheld no significant change, and yet... Were her breasts slightly fuller? She touched them, and to her amazement, they were tender. When had that happened?

Was her tummy even the slightest bit rounded? There, right below her navel. She stroked the soft spot, then jerked her hands away because it tickled.

And because for a second she could almost imagine her baby's heartbeat.

She smiled. The heartbeat of her child. What a wondrous sound it must— She caught sight of the clock and realized her ten minutes were almost up. With one more glance at her changing body, she hurried to her closet and slipped into a pair of sapphire blue silk lounging pants and matching tunic-length top. Perfect, she decided. Great color, and not too casual.

Now, if she could just act casual.

Cade was at the foot of the stairs. "I was about to come looking for you."

"Sorry."

"Don't be. It was worth the wait. You look..." He wanted to say "breathtaking" because that's exactly what had happened when he looked up and saw her coming down the stairs like an angel floating on a cloud. She had taken his breath away. "Fantastic."

"Thanks. What's that I smell?"

"Part of your surprise. Ready?"

She smiled, her eyes sparkling. "You bet."

He took her hand and led her into the den. There, in front of the big-screen television, was a mammoth bowl of popcorn, two soft drinks and two boxes of candy.

"What's this?"

"When I promise a girl a movie, I deliver." He walked over and popped a tape into the VCR. "The guy at the video store told me this was about a family of wine makers, set in the Napa Valley right after World War II. I thought you might like it."

Belle was so touched her eyes misted. "That was very thoughtful, Cade."

"It's, uh, called *A Walk in the Clouds.* Have you seen it?"

"No, but I heard it's very good."

Cade went over to the sofa and fluffed a couple of cushions. "There. Front-row seats."

She sat down and curled her bare feet beneath her. "Looks like you've thought of everything. When did you have time to pop the corn?"

"All right, you caught me. I cheated. They sold it in bags at the video store."

The gesture was so touching. He could have handed her the moon and it couldn't have meant more to her. Belle had an overwhelming urge to fling her arms around his neck and kiss him. The urge was so strong she clasped her hands together in her lap to keep from acting on it. She smiled. "Very thoughtful."

"Can't have a movie without popcorn." He hit the Start button on the remote control, and the title sequence began.

He passed her the popcorn bowl, and in the process moved even closer to her on the wide sofa. He held his breath for a second or two, waiting to see if she would reestablish the distance between them. She didn't, and Cade gave a mental shout. *Yes!*

The film had progressed for about fifteen minutes when Cade began to realize he had made a mistake listening to that punk at the video store. A serious mistake.

Belle almost choked on a mouthful of popcorn when the weepy heroine of the film announced to the hero that she was pregnant, unmarried and couldn't face her family. The next second she did choke when the hero offered to be the girl's make-believe husband.

# 8

"YOU ALL RIGHT?" Cade asked, slapping her on the back.

"Must have—" she reached for her Coke and took a big gulp "—gone down the wrong way."

"No joke," he mumbled, wondering how in the hell they were going to make it through this movie. In fact, he was wondering why she hadn't already called a halt to the whole evening.

Belle took another drink. "I'm fine now."

The word *awkward* didn't even begin to cover the situation, but not knowing what else to do, they resumed watching the movie.

With all the choking and patting, they had moved closer together. Cade's left arm was stretched across the back of the sofa, and Belle realized if she turned slightly and relaxed totally, she would practically be leaning against his chest. Not that the idea didn't have merit. She tried to concentrate on the screen instead of Cade's nearness, but that was even worse.

The heroine, in a nightgown, and the hero, in an old-fashioned sleeveless undershirt, were in a vineyard at night, trying to keep the frost from ruining the grape crop. Wearing framed, silk-covered "wings" on their arms—the kind she had heard her grandfather talk about—they fanned heat from smudge pots, the man standing so close behind the woman that his wings occasionally brushed her body.

Cade had stopped wondering why Belle hadn't told him to get the hell out, because his heart was beating so fast, so loud, he wouldn't have heard her, anyway. He was about ready to jump out of his skin. And when her knee accidentally brushed against his leg, he clenched his jaw, fighting the urge to pick up the remote control and throw it at the screen. He couldn't do this. He'd be dead by the time the movie was over.

He jerked his hand from the back of the sofa and reached for the remote control. "Listen, Belle, I'm sorry. I had no idea what this story was about or—"

She turned toward him, and the tip of her breast grazed his arm.

That's all he could take. He shot up from the sofa. "This wasn't such a good idea. I think I better—"

"No. It was a wonderful idea."

"But maybe we should try it again. With another movie. They had one of those Schwarzenegger flicks. You know, lots of action and—"

"I like this one."

He stared at her. "You like it?"

"Yes. And I'd like to see how it ends."

"You would?"

"Yes."

For more reasons than he knew. Even though it was fiction, she needed to know that the characters found a way to work out their problems. Suddenly it was very important for her to know there was a happy ending.

Cade didn't have to be hit between the eyes with a baseball bat to understand why she wanted to see the end. Their situation was so similar to the story—except for the pregnancy, of course—that it was scary. Knowing she was interested in how the movie ended, despite the fact that she had to be uncomfortable, gave him hope.

If she could stick it out, so could he. Who knows? Maybe the screenwriter could give them some ideas. He cooled his jets, took a deep breath and rejoined her on the sofa. As he did, he made an attitude adjustment, reminding himself that he was in this for the long haul. What he felt for Belle was too important to be overshadowed by mere lust.

Several times during the rest of the film, fatigue almost claimed her, but Belle fought the drowsiness. This time with Cade was too precious.

"That wasn't bad," he said when the movie ended.

"I loved it." *I love you,* she wanted to say.

"Good. Now I don't have to go back and strangle that guy at the video store."

Belle laughed, leaning her head back against the

sofa, against him. Cade moved his outstretched arm and pulled her closer. "You don't laugh enough."

"I had almost forgotten how," she said, sighing. "Cade?" Her gaze slid away from his.

"Yeah."

"Last night I realized that I'd been living in a rage for a long time. I also realized I've been unfair to you."

"Unfair?"

"When I asked you to...when I offered you our deal, I was ninety-nine percent sure you wouldn't turn it down."

"So?"

"So, I took advantage of you, and I...well, my perspective has changed."

His gut tightened. This sounded suspiciously like she was going to offer him a way out, and he wasn't ready to make his move yet. And he damned sure had no intention of walking away from her.

"Do I look like a pushover to you?"

"No, but—"

"Darlin', stop worrying about me. I can take care of myself."

"But, Cade—"

"You talk too much." He shut her up the best way he knew how.

He kissed her, softly, murmuring his satisfaction as her lips parted. He watched her lashes flutter closed, felt her sigh into his mouth. So warm. So sweet.

Belle melted against him, loving the way her body
fit to his. Loving the feel, the taste, the texture of this
man. Never in her life had she felt so peaceful, so totally secure. She pulled back, but only to lay her head
on his shoulder and listen to his heartbeat keeping
time with hers. She was so relaxed, so comfortable,
she couldn't keep her eyes open.

Cade held her close. "Listen, Belle, I've been thinking that maybe we got a better deal than either of us
realized. Hell, in the beginning, I only had one thing
on my mind. Not that I'm proud of that. I'm not. But
I've wanted you for so long."

He took a deep breath, preparing to spill the rest of
his guts, and realized she hadn't moved a muscle in
the last ten seconds.

"Belle?" No response. "Belle?" He looked down
and discovered she was sound asleep.

"Poor baby." He kissed her temple, then picked
her up and carried her upstairs. He put her to bed in
her room, then once again he lay down beside her, on
top of the covers. Tonight he took off his shirt before
he pulled her into his arms and pillowed her head on
his shoulder. He thought briefly about removing her
shirt, then changed his mind. She might not be
thrilled with that tomorrow morning. Besides, the
silk was so thin he could feel the rise and fall of her
breasts against his chest as she breathed. It was
enough. But when he slept, his dreams were of more.
A lot more.

BELLE WAS DISAPPOINTED when she woke up and found Cade gone. The morning sun streamed in, making her feel all lazy and languid, like a cat sunning itself, and it would have been so delicious to curl up next to him. Thank goodness she had no early appointments, because she wasn't sure she could get out of bed right now if the house was on fire. Yawning, she rolled onto her back and tucked her hands behind her head, thinking dreamily of the night before. She couldn't remember when she'd felt so happy.

Falling asleep in his arms was becoming a habit. Not that she was complaining. He had great arms, a great body, a positively wicked smile, and she loved the way his hazel eyes sparkled.

Belle thought about the characteristics her child might inherit. Between Cade's all-American good looks and her Italian ancestry, their children would be handsome. She imagined a little girl with curls the color of rich cocoa and eyes the color of toffee. Or a little boy with tawny blond hair and dark brown eyes. Beautiful children, happy and loved.

A wonderful picture, but would it include a loving father?

She couldn't put off telling him about the baby much longer, but she knew the minute he found out, the surprises, the sweet talk and the even sweeter kisses would end.

And she didn't want that.

To be honest, she wanted the fantasy, the dream. She wanted him to love her and the child she was carrying, and make a real home for them. But, unfortunately, reality had an ugly way of intruding on dreams.

He might not want her or the baby. He might not even want her to keep it. If he wasn't ready to be a father, she wouldn't hold him, but this baby would be born. Daddy or no daddy.

She had known from the beginning that Cade wasn't the kind of man who thought about settling down. Whenever he left Sweetwater Springs, the notion that he might be out having a high old time crossed her mind more than once. She had all but given him her blessing to sleep around, for crying out loud. Of course, that was before she knew she loved him. Her only solace was Reese's confident statement the day she found out Cade was back.

*Cade McBride never went back on a deal in his life. When he makes a promise, he doesn't break it. Ever.*

Did that mean he had been faithful to their marriage vows during the six weeks he was gone? She wanted to believe he had. She wanted to believe it so badly, she ached.

But what if he didn't believe she had kept their vows? What if he thought this child belonged to another man? Could fate be that cruel? Of course it could. Look what had already happened. She had paid Cade to marry her, thinking she could set him aside like an old shoe, but he refused to be ignored. She'd gone into their deal on a strictly business basis and had ended up head over heels in love. Now she was pregnant. When she told him, it would serve her right if he turned his back on the whole thing. The land, the marriage, her and the baby.

Belle sighed, her happiness of moments ago gone. Logic insisted that she had to tell him, she thought as she headed to the bathroom for a shower. Putting it off only made matters worse.

She could do it.

After all, she was a big girl, and if she wasn't, then it was certainly time for her to grow up.

Yeah, she could do this.

Stepping beneath the stinging spray, she let the water beat down on her tense shoulders, flowing over her until her skin tingled.

Sure she could.

She shut off the water, toweled herself dry, then slipped into a robe. Tonight, after work, she would tell him. She had all day to build up her courage, and it would take every minute. Then the worst of it would be behind her.

Yeah, right.

The worst would be when Cade walked out of her life. Only this time, he wouldn't be back. Belle didn't doubt for a minute that he was honorable enough to make sure he provided for his child, but that wouldn't include the baby's mother. He might even be gone by tomorrow.

Standing in her bedroom, staring at the rumpled covers where Cade had slept, she wanted to cry, scream or throw something. None of which would get her what she wanted.

Cade. Her thoughts drifted to the night they married. Cade. Awakening the passion she had kept locked inside herself for so many years. Cade. Loving her, giving her more than anyone ever had.

Cade, Cade, Cade...

Her feelings for him had taken over her mind, her heart, maybe even her soul. Doing the right thing was no longer relevant balanced against her need for him. Love and logic weren't synonymous. Reason rarely directs the heart. The only certainty was her love for him.

She wanted another night like their wedding night. And, she decided, right or wrong, fair or not, she was going to have it.

"YOU SURE THIS IS GOING to work, ace?"

"Tomorrow morning, all you have to do," Cade told Reese, "is say that you dropped by the ranch office and Dorothy Fielding mentioned the quarterly report."

They were in the barn, and Cade was working on some tack. "What if it's not ready? Tomorrow is Saturday," Reese reminded him.

Cade thought for a minute, then finally resigned himself to the obvious. "Guess we'll have to wait until Monday. What choice do we have?"

"You know, I've been thinking. The way you and I have been bird-doggin' Carrington, he hasn't had any time to get rid of those horses."

"Which means he's probably got a place close by where he can hold them until he can move them."

"You think he's selling them to one of those big spreads in Mexico?"

"Thinking of those babies improving somebody's bloodline is better than thinking they went to killers for dog food," Cade said.

"We should call the sheriff's office and tell them what you found."

Cade had discovered that an old trailer stuck on a back lot for more than a week, with three flat tires, had been repaired and driven. The wheels were still covered in the red mud of the caprock. The same kind of mud he had found on the axle of Carrington's truck. Not exactly solid proof, but it was a start.

"I suppose, but I sure would like to catch him red-handed."

Reese nodded. "Better still, find out where he's stashed his booty. Too bad we have to wait until Monday. I wouldn't mind seeing that sleaze behind bars tomorrow."

"I'm with you there. But, tomorrow or Monday, the plan is the same. You pick up the report, then, loyal employee and friend that you are, you offer to bring the report to Belle. You did say she always reads them?"

"Always."

Cade picked up a bridle that needed repair, examined it for a few seconds, then set it aside for later. "Once she sees the count is different from the last quarter, she'll figure out the rest. Belle is too smart to overlook a detail like that. She'll want answers. And that's where you come in."

"With the news of the other thefts."

"Right. Then shift the conversation toward ranch hands who might have drifted in and out in the last few weeks, and...anybody new in the area. If I know my smart little cookie, she'll peg Carrington faster than a bull out of the shoot."

Reese shoved his hat back on his head. "Do you ever plan on telling her about your part in this?"

"No. I want her to feel that she handled this all on her own."

Reese looked at his friend. "You really do love her, don't you?"

"Yes."

"I didn't think I'd ever live to see the day you settled down." Pause. "You are thinking about settling down, aren't you? I mean marriage."

"In case you've forgotten, we're already married."

"I mean for real."

"Yeah. For real. That's why it's important she feels like she's taking care of this herself."

Reese thought for a moment, trying to decide whether or not to share his observations regarding the stress Belle had been under since taking over the winery. He wasn't sure it would help, but it sure wouldn't hurt. "She's walking a tightrope, and doing a damned fine job, I might add. But it hasn't been easy."

"I know that. And I'm hoping that she'll offer me my old job. That way I can take some of the worry off her shoulders."

"I hope this works."

"Trust me, I know what I'm doing."

"That's probably what Dillinger said just before they gunned him down. And we both know Belle is a good shot."

"Don't remind me."

"Something to think about, ace." Reese grinned and walked to his truck.

Cade waved as he drove off. This was going to work. And once it was all over, probably tomorrow, he would put all his skills—and they were considerable, if he did say so himself—into seducing Belle. And this time, she would *know* it was for real.

Yeah, this was going to work.

Carrington would get what was coming to him, and Belle would be the heroine. He didn't see a single flaw in the plan.

BELLE HAD NEVER SET OUT to deliberately seduce a man before, and she hoped nothing went wrong with her plan. She was usually so preoccupied with her work that she ordered most of her clothes through catalogs. But this time, her grand scheme called for personal attention. She left work early to do a little shopping and surprised herself by thoroughly enjoying it. Now she was on her way home, intending to have a leisurely shower, slip into the decadent new nightgown she had just purchased, and then... Then what? She had to admit, at this point her plan sort of fell apart.

Maybe she shouldn't hit him with sexy lingerie right off the bat. Maybe a good dinner, some soft music, a little wine...

No, that wouldn't work. She couldn't drink because of the baby, and he would be sure to notice. The whole purpose of her plan was to have one more night together before he found out about his impending fatherhood.

Okay, Isabella, think. You can do this.

Dinner is good. Soft music works. Then maybe just let nature take its course? Why not, she thought. It worked the first time.

When she arrived home, the house was quiet. Great, she had some time to herself. She set her briefcase on the table in the foyer as usual, tucked her package under her arm and went upstairs. Fifteen minutes later she came out of the shower feeling re-

freshed. Nervous, but refreshed. Now to see if the ris-
qué lingerie looked as alluring on her as it had on the
mannequin in the store. Belle shrugged off her robe,
lifted the lid on the box and removed the silky confec-
tion from beneath fancy tissue paper. Then she
slipped it over her head.

The cream-colored silk drifted down her body,
swaying, settling around her like moonlight on night-
blooming jasmine. With thin straps and a neckline
that left very little to the imagination, it was the most
deliciously daring thing she had ever owned. And
she loved it. Raising the hem of the gown, she
waltzed around, enjoying the feel of the silk as it
swirled around her bare legs. She was so enthralled
with herself, she almost missed the sound of someone
coming down the hall.

"Posey? Is that you?"

"That's the second time you've mistaken me for
Posey. Maybe you need your eyes—"

Cade stood there, stunned.

Embarrassed, Belle didn't know if she should cross
her arms over her chest or make a mad dash for her
robe. In the end, she simply stood there. "I thought I
was...I didn't know you were..."

"God, you're beautiful."

At his praise her embarrassment dissolved into excitement. A tingling skittered along her nerves until
her skin felt hot. This was what she wanted. Maybe

not as she had planned, but the results would be the same. They would be together.

"Tell me I'm dreaming," he said, moving closer. "Tell me I'm having one of my millions of fantasies about you, because if this is real, I'm in deep trouble."

"Do you want it to be real?"

He stopped and stared at her. "Like I want my next breath. No, I take that back. I'd gladly give up my next breath to know this is real. That you're standing there in that...that—"

"Nightgown."

"Waiting for me to take it off you."

Her legs were threatening to give way any second, and her body was trembling so much, it was a wonder he couldn't hear the silk rustling against her skin.

"I'm waiting."

His gaze shot to hers. "What?"

"I'm waiting. I think I've been waiting for you—for this, since the moment you came back."

"But I thought—"

"That I would fight you. I know." She felt fragile and nervous, like being caught in a summer thunderstorm without anywhere to run. At the same time, strength surged through her, making her feel powerful enough to conquer the world. "Why should I fight something I want so much?"

"God, Belle, this is killing me. We can't."

"But you just said—"

"That I want you, and I do. But, darlin', I'm not

prepared. I don't have anything with me, and we can't take a chance."

"Don't worry." She touched his cheek. "I've...I'm protected."

"Sure?"

She nodded. "There's no risk of me getting pregnant tonight."

Relieved, Cade closed his eyes briefly. "I've wanted you—wanted this—for so long." He captured her wrists and turned her palm up to receive his lips. "Baby, you're shaking. Are you afraid?"

She managed a breathy laugh. "Only that you'll stop."

His fingers still around her wrist, he pulled her into his arms. "No chance." He touched his mouth to hers, tasting, stroking. "I need you too bad to stop."

He needed her. Belle thought her heart would gallop out of her chest. "That night...I didn't know it could be like that. I felt so free, so...wild."

"Like a gypsy princess." He kissed her throat, then his lips traveled down to the swell of her breasts. "I've relived that night in my dreams a thousand times. But this is better."

She pushed her hands through his hair, forcing him to look into her eyes. "Make me wild again, Cade."

His mouth came down hard on hers, feasting, devouring. She met him stroke for stroke, need for need. With his mouth still clinging to hers, he worked the buttons of his shirt free and pulled it off. When she reached for the straps of her gown, he stopped her.

"Let me...please."

The "please" undid her, unraveled her tentative hold on what was left of her sanity. "Yes. Touch me. The way you touched me before."

"No. Not like before."

"But—"

"This time will be different. I've thought about this for weeks. Dreamed about it." He hooked a finger under one thin strap and tugged. "I don't want fast and furious. This time I want to see the pleasure in your eyes, feel it in your body." He tugged the other strap free. Two things prevented the skimpy bodice from sliding to her hips. He reached out and touched her nipples. The bodice collapsed, leaving her breasts bared to his ravenous gaze. Her eyes went wild and dark, passion dancing in their depths like devils dancing before leaping flames.

"I want to look into your eyes as I slip inside you. Then I want to stroke you slowly until the fire burns out of control." He kissed the swell of each breast, her throat, her mouth.

Belle gave herself over to the kiss, the desire rushing through her body so fast, so hot, it was almost painful. And when his tongue did wonderfully wicked, and blatantly carnal, things, her head spun. For all she cared, the world was spinning off its axis. She grabbed his shoulders and hung on.

"Oh, God," he whispered. "Does that feel as good to you as it does to me?"

Emotion clogged her throat to the point that she could barely assure him. "Yes. Oh, yes." More. She wanted more, needed more. She wasn't sure she could ever get enough.

Without realizing it, they had moved backward to the bed. He put his hand to the small of her back and pushed the gown over her hips. As it fell to the floor, he lowered her to the bed and reached for the snap of his jeans at the same time. In two seconds he was free of the denim and his briefs.

They were naked together. Gloriously, completely, flesh to flesh.

Cade trailed his fingers from her ankle to her waist, across the satin smoothness of her tummy. "That night. I didn't take the time to appreciate how beautiful you are. I'm sorry—"

She put her finger to his mouth. "No regrets. I wouldn't change anything about that night except..."

"What?"

"That it ended too soon."

"We'll make up for lost time."

He kissed her, patiently, erotically, driving all thought from her head but how much she wanted him. And she poured everything she had into the kiss, needing him to know the strength and depth of her desire for him. When he lowered his head to her breasts, closing his mouth over a hardened nipple, she gasped with pleasure and bucked under him.

Her response almost sent him over the edge, and he fought to keep from plunging into her, taking the heat she offered, the heat he so desperately needed. But he reminded himself this was about a need much deeper than physical pleasure. Slowly, he caressed her, finally moving his hand to cup the heat between her thighs.

She tried to make another sound, but at the first stroke of his fingers, she couldn't speak, couldn't do anything but ride the wave of pleasure until it crested, throwing her up on the shore of a shattering climax. Eyes closed, she tried to reach for him, but her hands slid away, boneless.

"Look at me." As he pulled her beneath him, she opened her eyes. Slowly at first, then wider as he slipped inside her.

She arched her back, taking him deep. They moved slowly at first, prolonging the pleasure. But soon she was pleading with him to end the sweet burning, the ache only he could satisfy. Faster and deeper they hurled themselves toward the oblivion that was both darkness and light, pain and joy. At the end, they called out each other's names and tumbled over the edge together.

THERE WAS NO disappointment when Belle woke that morning, because Cade was right beside her. And he wasn't on top of the covers. She snuggled close as he opened his eyes.

"Good morning."

He kissed her mouth softly. "I was beginning to think I would have to sleep in my clothes forever."

Belle smiled against his lips. "Took us long enough, didn't it."

He wrapped his arms around her. "It was worth the wait."

"I'll say."

He lifted a wave of dark hair from her shoulder and nuzzled her throat. "You're one helluva woman, you know that? Smart, sexy. Passionate."

For him. Only for him. She ran her hands over his back and shoulders, loving the feel, the taste of his skin. "I've never thought of myself as sexy."

"Well, you'd better start, because you are. I haven't been able to think about anything else but how you feel, how you smell. You've been driving me out of my mind ever since I dodged that .22 bullet."

Belle winced. "I'm sorry about that."

"Why? You were right. I was a jerk."

"No, you weren't."

Cade lifted his head and gazed into her eyes. "Darlin', I was a class A knot head. I was so hot for you, I couldn't think straight. But that's no excuse. I should have—"

She kissed him hard. "I don't care about then. 'Now' is what's important. Here, and now." She reached under the sheet to stroke him. He was already hard.

Cade groaned. "Are you trying to kill me?"

"I'm trying to show you how much I want you."

He rolled her over and under him. "I get the picture," he said, driving his point home.

In minutes they were sailing off the edge of the world again.

The next time she opened her eyes, he was just coming out of the bathroom.

"Hey, gorgeous." He walked over to the bed and kissed her.

"Oh, I'll bet. I probably look like the Wicked Witch of the West. Is my hair sticking up everywhere?"

"I say you're gorgeous, so you're gorgeous."

"Hmm." She scooted deeper into the folds of the sheet. "You need coffee to get your eyes open."

Cade took her chin in his hand. "My eyes are wide open," he said in a solemn voice. "Belle, we need to talk."

The word *talk* made her remember she had yet to face him with her news. "Yes, I guess we do."

"I'll be tied up until almost five. Can we have dinner together?"

What was a few more hours? "Sure."

He grinned. "Give me a kiss I can think about all day."

Belle rose up, threw her arms around his neck and kissed him as if it were the last time.

"Whoa, darlin'. More of that and I won't be able to ride a horse, much less break one." He walked to the bedroom door, gave a wave and left.

That's when Belle realized she had truly gone insane. And on top of that she was a coward. A greedy coward.

Too greedy to give up the fantasy just yet.

She didn't want to talk. She wanted more of what they had shared last night. Okay, so she was a wimp. Yes, putting it off was undoubtedly a mistake. She could add it to the growing list. And no, she wasn't sticking her head in the sand. She was just desperately hanging on to a dream.

She fretted all day about her lack of backbone. If her grandfather were still alive, he would have wagged a finger at her and said, "For shame, Bella. You must do what is right." But then, if he were still alive, she wouldn't be facing this problem. The irony of ironies, she thought.

Cade called late in the afternoon. "Hello, gorgeous."

Just the sound of his voice brightened her whole world. "I've got a better shot at it than the last time you saw me."

"The last time I saw you, you looked like you had just made wild, passionate love."

She sighed. "I had."

"Oh, yeah."

There was a lengthy pause. "You still there?" she asked.

"I'm remembering that little sound you make the first instant I'm inside you."

Her breath hitched. "No fair."

"What's the matter? Cat got your tongue?"

"I can't...talk at the moment."

"You can listen." And he proceeded to tell her all the things he wanted to do to her when they were alone. All the ways he wanted to touch her, stroke her. His voice was deep, barely above a whisper and erotically thrilling. His words were naughty and wildly arousing.

"Stop," she hissed. "You're driving me—"

"Wild?"

"You know you are."

"I like you that way."

"Yes, but you're not here to, uh..."

"Appreciate it?"

"Exactly. And since I have at least another hour of work to finish before we can—"

"Continue our conversation."

"Uh, yes."

"Okay, then, I better let you go. We can *talk* later."

How could one word sound so seductive? "Did anyone ever tell you, McBride, that you're a tease?"

"No, McBride, but we'll discuss that, too."

After she hung up, Belle simply stared at the

phone. She should be ashamed of her cowardice, but at the moment, she was having trouble calming her racing heart, much less facing her guilt.

# 9

"WOW," BELLE SAID when she caught sight of Cade at the front door.

Wearing a pair of black jeans that fit so well they were a threat to the heartbeat of any female within fifty miles, and a green-and-black western shirt, he looked fantastic.

"Thank you, ma'am." He took her hand, managing to relieve her of her briefcase and pull her into his arms at the same time. "Got a date with my wife." His mouth came down on hers in a deliciously welcoming kiss.

"Lucky woman," Belle said when they broke the kiss.

"Lucky, but late. Go change."

"Why?"

"I asked you out to dinner, remember? Besides, I've already made reservations."

"Oh." In truth, she hadn't remembered. Working up the nerve to share her "little news" hadn't left much room in her thoughts for anything else. On top of that, she was exhausted.

"Cade, you don't have to take me out. I wouldn't mind having a nice, relaxing dinner here."

"Nope. I'm taking you out, and that's final. I want to show you off. Let the world see what a lucky guy *I* am."

Belle knew she wasn't unattractive, but her looks had never been something she thought much about one way or the other. Her parents and grandparents had always stressed inner, rather than outer, beauty. No one had ever wanted to "show her off." Only Cade. That, combined with the easy way he referred to her as his wife, had her close to tears. How could she refuse him?

She kissed him on the cheek. "I won't be a minute."

An hour later, the world got a glimpse of the lucky man as he escorted his stunning wife into a restaurant called The Fifty Yard Line. The eatery was one of Lubbock's best and, despite its name, was definitely not a sports bar. The decor was rustic elegance with touches of classic football memorabilia of the past, mostly centered around the local university, Texas Tech, and teams of the Southwest Conference.

Cade and Belle were seated at an intimate corner table for two. Within minutes, it became clear to her that he had not only called ahead, but had requested special touches. Almost as soon as they sat down, a waiter brought them an appetizer of stuffed crab and mushrooms, and poured them a glass of wine from a bottle already chilling at the table.

Belle gazed at him. "You thought of everything."

He shrugged as if the whole setup was run-of-the-mill, but she knew better. "A little special treatment never hurt anybody."

Belle felt like the biggest fraud in the world sitting across from Cade, holding his hand as if she deserved all this wonderful attention he was lavishing on her.

Oh, God, what a tangled web she had woven for herself.

Cade raised his glass in a toast. "To us." When Belle lifted her water glass, he frowned. "Something wrong with the wine?"

"No, of course not." She smiled, hoping it didn't look strained. "What could be wrong? It's one of ours. No, I've got a little bit of a tension headache. Wine aggravates it."

"Darlin', you should have said something." Pause. "Well, hell, how big an idiot am I? You did. 'Cade, you don't have to take me out. I wouldn't mind a nice relaxing dinner at home.' It just didn't penetrate my thick skull."

One lie always leads to another, she thought. Now she was stuck with her "headache." "You had already made reservations, and I hated to disappoint you."

"But you've got to eat."

"I'm not hungry." That much, at least, was the truth.

"Thought we agreed no more skipping meals." Cade snagged the waiter's attention. "How about if I order something to go?"

In less than fifteen minutes, they were on their way back to the ranch. And when they got home, he made her eat at least half of the meal he'd ordered. Afterward, he massaged her neck and shoulders.

"You weren't kidding when you said tension."

"Hmm. That feels so good. I'm sorry I ruined your plans."

"You didn't ruin anything. We can go back anytime."

No, they couldn't, or at least, they wouldn't. Having to lie about the wine, then cover that lie with another, made her realize the longer she waited, the more lies she would have to tell. Sooner or later, one of them would trip her up. Probably sooner.

"Cade." She placed her hands over his, lifting them from her temples. But she didn't let go. "You told me this morning that you wanted to talk. I think we should."

He leaned down and kissed her neck. "Not tonight. I want you tension-free when we have our discussion. For now, I think you should get some rest."

She was good and truly caught in the tangled web of her own making. Either she played out the headache scenario or convinced him it was gone. Coward that she was, she took the easy way out. "All right."

He led her upstairs, helped her into her gown, then held the covers while she slipped beneath them. Minutes later he crawled in next to her and pulled her into his arms. Belle's sigh was part exhaustion mixed with pure contentment as she drifted into sleep.

Cade held her, savoring the feel of her in his arms. Moments like this, quiet and intimate, were the ones he looked forward to the most. They kept him going, kept him believing in the kind of love he had once thought impossible. Now he found it amazing that all of the notions of romance, all the poetry of emotion, were basically true. Love did hit you right between the eyes. It made you feel as if you were ten feet tall. And it aroused such feelings of protectiveness and devotion that you wanted to make the person you loved totally happy. Outside of all that, it simply was the most wonderful sensation on earth.

It didn't take much of an imagination to understand why the Good Lord had made man and woman to be together. Nothing in Cade's life had ever felt so right. The only thing that could make it better was knowing their marriage was real.

Cade smiled, thinking about the small but perfect diamond solitaire he had purchased earlier today. He had intended to give it to her tonight and ask her to marry him—again. He hoped they could start all over again, including another wedding, only in a church this time. The idea of saying his vows to Belle in front of God and all their friends would give him a sense of completion, yet renewal.

He sighed, snuggling closer to her. Oh, well, there

was no hurry. The ring was still in the pocket of his
jeans, and Belle was in his arms. It could wait.

Sometime during the night she awoke for no ap-
parent reason. Beside her, Cade was sleeping peace-
fully. As she watched him, a yearning pierced her
soul. A yearning not just for his embrace, but for the
sensation of wholeness she felt in his arms. She
couldn't stop herself from reaching for him, from
gently touching his shoulder.

He woke up immediately and rolled over. "Headache worse?"

She shook her head. "Hold me, Cade."

He slipped his arms around her and held her close,
kissing the temple he had massaged hours earlier.
Eventually, his kisses explored softer territory, her
earlobe, her throat, her lips. His tongue skimmed
along her full bottom lip, and she shivered. Predict-
ably, her response sent him the message he had been
waiting for. But tonight there was no hurry. Tonight
they stoked the flame of passion slowly, sweetly. And
when it ended, they snuggled, contented, lying together spoon fashion.

While Belle listened to Cade's even breathing, she
gave in to the heartbreak she knew was inevitable.
Tonight he hadn't made her wild for love. But un-
knowingly, he had made her weep for its loss.

WHEN SHE WOKE in the morning, he was just slipping
out the door. He turned and gave her one last smile,
then was gone.

One last smile.

For a moment, she thought about pulling the covers over her head and giving in to the dark depression tugging at her. But, of course, she wouldn't. She would get up, shower, dress and go into the office. But her heart wasn't in it. After today, she feared her heart would never be the same.

Cade was just coming downstairs when the doorbell rang. He opened it, expecting to find Reese, and he wasn't disappointed.

"You get it?" he asked as soon as the door closed.

Reese held up a computer printout.

"Great." He turned, sprinted up the stairs and back to the bedroom. The bed was empty, and the shower was running. He knocked on the bathroom door.

"Hey, darlin', Reese is here with the quarterly report."

"Tell him to put it in my briefcase," she called out over the rushing water.

"Will do."

"We're rolling," he said when he rejoined Reese. "She wants you to put it in her briefcase."

"I hope this doesn't come back and bite us both in the butt." Reese popped the twin latches on the attaché and opened it, but he didn't put the report inside.

"What? Don't mess around. Just throw it in there and—"

At the strange look on his friend's face, Cade stepped behind him, glanced down at the open brief-

case and saw what looked like a lab report from a
doctor's office, and on top of it were several pamphlets.

The top one was titled *The First Trimester of Pregnancy—Options and Concerns.*

"Cade—"

He cut Reese off with a wave of his hand. "Close
it."

"But—"

"Close it. Put the quarterly report on top."

Reese did as Cade instructed, then turned to say
something, anything that might lessen the shock of
what they had just seen. "Listen, ace..."

The front door was standing wide open, and he
was talking to thin air.

At the ranch office, Dorothy Fielding looked up as
Tom Carrington walked through the door.

"Good morning, Dorothy."

"Tom." She didn't much care for the foreman, but
it wasn't in her to be rude. "Was there something you
needed?"

"Thought I'd take a look at the quarterly report,
then carry it over to Mrs. McBride."

"Nice of you to offer, but Reese beat you to it."

"What do you mean?"

"He was in about ten minutes ago, and took the extra copy. Said he was going to the house, anyway,
and it saved me some steps."

"You got another copy?"

"Just the one already filed. I can run another off the printer if you—"

"Never mind." The foreman turned and strode out the door, leaving it to bang behind him.

BELLE WAS PREGNANT. *Pregnant!*

The word kept stomping around in Cade's brain like a herd of rampaging elephants. His head hurt from the pressure. But it was nothing compared to his heart.

She'd lied to him. He'd asked her straight out, and she had lied to him.

Walking toward the round pen, he looked down at his chest, half expecting to see a knife sticking out of his heart and blood running down the front of his shirt. The pain was like nothing he'd ever felt in his life. Nothing. White-hot, it cut into his heart, slicing it into little pieces. Painful, betrayed little pieces.

For an instant, just a heartbeat, when he had realized what the brochures meant, a joy so pure, so sweet had filled his soul. The next second he had tumbled headlong into an abyss of pain.

Reese caught up with him at the round pen.

"Stay away from me." Cade's fist hit the top rail of the pen, spooking the horse waiting to be worked. "I need to put my fist through something solid."

"Easy, ace. You want to punch something, start with me."

"How could she keep something like that from me?" Suddenly he whipped around, eyes narrowed, his body almost in a fighting stance. "You didn't know, did you?"

"No! Lord, no."

His shoulders sagged. "That's something, at least."

"Cade, did it occur to you that maybe she just found out? Maybe she was just trying to find the right moment to tell you?"

"We've spent the past three nights together. We made love. We talked. She had plenty of *moments*, Reese. Plenty of time to tell me. Why didn't she?"

"I don't know. But you can't go off like a Roman candle."

It was a testimony to Cade's control and, whether he believed it now or not, his faith in Belle that he hadn't voiced the thought that the baby might not be his, Reese thought. "I'm sure she's got good reasons."

"What reasons? What reasons could she have not to tell me she was carrying my baby?"

"Talk to her."

He paced back and forth in front of the pen. "Not now."

"Of course not. You're too angry." Too hurt, he could have added. "Cool down, okay? Then you can go to her and talk it out."

He kept pacing. "Yeah, you're probably right."

"I know I'm right."

Cade stopped pacing. "The hell you are." And he took off for the house.

While Cade was making his way to the house, Belle was preparing to leave. The doorbell rang as her foot touched the bottom stair. She opened the door to find Tom Carrington.

"Tom?"

"Mornin', Mrs. McBride. Wasn't sure if you'd already gone to the office or not."

"I was just on my way. Is there a problem?"

"Yes'm, I believe so."

At his hesitation, Belle frowned. "Well?"

"I'm just not sure how to say this, Mrs. McBride. Don't like to accuse anyone of stealing, but—"

"Stealing?"

He nodded. "I've suspected feed theft for the last couple of weeks, but couldn't catch anybody. But the quarterly is out, and it pretty much confirms we're short four babies."

Belle remembered thinking the number hadn't sounded right to her the day she ran into Cade at the round pen, but she had dismissed it from her thoughts. "When was the last time they were counted?"

"Two, maybe two and a half months ago."

"Who was responsible for the tally?"

Belle regretted the question even before it was out of her mouth. Two months ago Cade was foreman.

"McBride."

"Well, who did the actual counting? It's possible someone reported the wrong number—"

"If you check the printout, his initials are in the job number-ID column."

Belle retrieved the printout from her briefcase and flipped through it until she found the correct entry. Sure enough, Cade's initials indicated he was the employee who had taken a physical count of the horses on the open range.

"What exactly are you trying to say, Tom?"

"All I know is, since he showed up, we're short four horses and a lot of feed."

The foreman shifted his weight from one foot to the other and back. He was nervous. And he damned well had cause. The man was all but accusing her husband of being a horse thief.

"And?" Belle said, realizing he was enjoying feeding her one tidbit of information after the other.

"That double trailer that's been on the back lot, the one with three flat tires."

"I know the one you mean."

"I sent one of the boys down there this morning to fix the flat tires, but someone had already done it. And it's been moved."

He was so obvious. "You think Cade used that trailer to steal our horses?"

"Yes, ma'am. And as hard as it might be for you to hear this, Mrs. McBride, I don't think it's coincidence that this started happening just when your husband comes back."

"That's ridiculous! Cade's not a thief. Besides, he was foreman for over three years and nothing was ever stolen."

"That you know of."

"You're way off base, Tom. I know Cade. What reason on earth would he have for stealing from me?"

"If you'll excuse me for saying so, ma'am, revenge."

"Revenge?"

"It's no secret you ran him off once."

"But that had nothing to do with—"

"And there's been talk that he sweet-talked you into getting married so he could have control over everything. I figure a man like McBride would be pretty ticked if he got bounced from such a sweet deal. Maybe ticked enough to want to get back at you."

Now he had gone too far. A cold fury shimmered through Belle. "Not only are you wrong, Tom, you've insulted my intelligence." In the back of her mind, she remembered having similar thoughts when Cade had returned, but that was before she knew him. Before she could deal with her own insecurities. If Tom thought Cade had been stringing her along, trying to gain her trust so he could steal right under her nose, obviously the foreman had little respect for her judgment.

"You must think I'm incompetent, or at least so

love struck I can't see straight. And how I could have missed such a condescending attitude when I interviewed you, I'll never know. Draw your pay, Tom. I want you out of the bunkhouse and gone by the end of—"

The front door burst open so hard it slammed back against the wall. Cade stormed through the doorway, glaring at Belle. "I want to talk to you."

Shocked at the cold fury in his eyes, she took a step back. "Cade—"

"You can't come in here causing trouble, Mc-Bride," Carrington warned.

In midstride Cade whirled on the foreman. "And you're not far down on my list. You worthless son of a bitch, I'm going to nail your sorry butt—"

"Cade! What's gotten into you?"

"Me?" he roared, turning back to her.

At that moment, Reese came through the doorway. "Calm down, ace." He glanced at the foreman. "What's he doing here?"

"S-somebody's stealing," Belle tried to explain, her eyes still on Cade. "There are some babies missing, and Tom thinks he knows who...who..." She put her hand to her mouth as if to prevent the words from escaping.

Cade's gaze drilled her. "He told you *I* stole those horses?"

Because they were in the center of the drama, the

three of them scarcely noticed Tom Carrington slinking out the door.

"Yes, but—"

"And you believed him?"

"No! Of course not. You're the most honest person I've ever met."

"Too bad we can't say the same about you, can we, darlin'? Isn't there something you've conveniently forgotten to tell me? A tiny little item that just slipped your mind."

He knew!

Belle's eyes widened, and her hand fell limply at her side.

"You've manipulated and bargained from day one so you could have your precious winery. That's all you care about, isn't it?"

She shook her head.

"Oh, yes, it is. You don't care about me, or my baby."

She didn't know how he knew, but he did. And he wasn't ever going to forgive her. That, too, was in his eyes, along with the rage. The world came crashing down around her shoulders, and all she could do was stand there while it happened. She was rooted to the spot, her gaze fastened on Cade's face.

"Ace," Reese said calmly, putting a hand on his friend's shoulder. Cade shrugged it off.

"I asked you point-blank the day I came back, and you lied to me."

"No, I—I didn't know for sure—"

"How long? How long have you known, Belle?"

She looked into his eyes and saw nothing but con-
demnation. She squared her shoulders, knowing he
must have the truth. Even if knowing the truth meant
his leaving. "Two days."

"How far along—"

"Six weeks, five days and—" she glanced at the
grandfather clock "—and ten hours." It was her way
of telling him there was no way the baby could be another man's, but he wasn't listening. Or didn't care.

"And I suppose you plan to get rid of it, just like
you plan to get rid of me once I'm no longer useful."

Belle closed her eyes so he couldn't see her pain.
"No, I'm...I'm keeping it."

Until that moment, Cade hadn't realized how
scared he had been that she might not have the baby.
From the moment he had seen the lab report and
pamphlets in her briefcase, the horror that she might
not want his child had clutched at his heart with icy
talons. The oppressive hold on his heart eased
slightly.

"When were you planning to tell me?"

She opened her eyes and looked directly at him. As
much as she hadn't wanted him to see her pain moments ago, she clutched at the hope that now he
might see how much she loved him. It was there in
her eyes, if only he would look. "Last night."

"Why didn't you?"

He didn't see her love. He didn't want to see it.

Belle shook her head. "It doesn't matter." And it didn't. He wouldn't believe her now.

Reese had taken several steps back, but stayed. He had never seen Cade like this, and to be honest, he wasn't sure what might happen.

"It might not matter to you, but it matters to me."

"Damn!" Reese said, noticing Carrington was gone.

Cade glanced around. "Aw, hell. Call the sheriff's department."

As Reese went to make the call, Cade turned back to Belle.

"Satisfied? Now half the county is going to have to clean up your mistake. This isn't over by a long shot. I've got a lot of questions that need answers, and—"

"They're on their way," Reese said, stepping back into the foyer.

Cade thought for a moment. "He'll probably head toward Levelland, then over the state line to New Mexico."

"There's a lot of open country between here and the state line. He could take any of a dozen side roads and be out of reach in an hour."

"You're telling me. I'm going after him."

"Cade, that's crazy," Reese insisted.

Behind him he heard Belle gasp, but he ignored it. "Hey, I'm not risking my hide for that jerk, but this way I can keep his truck in sight and use the CB to call in his position."

"Then, I'm going with you."

"Thanks, but you need to fill the cops in. Stay on channel seven, and I'll contact you."

"Be careful, ace."

Cade turned to Belle. "I'll be back, so don't go any-where. I mean it, Belle. I want you here when I return. We *will* talk."

Stunned, Belle watched as Cade disappeared through the open doorway. "H-he'll be all right, won't he, Reese? He won't do anything—"

"He'll be fine." But Reese wasn't sure she would be. She was shaking like a leaf in a stiff breeze, and her face was almost colorless. When she swayed, then grabbed hold of the edge of the foyer table, he rushed to her side.

"Belle, maybe you better sit down. I've got to go to the office and use the base station so I can stay in con-tact with Cade."

"I'm...all right."

"You sure?"

"Yes, and you don't have to go to the office. There's a CB in my Suburban."

He grabbed for her purse. "Where are your car keys?"

"Inside pocket." Steadier now, she took the purse, reached her hand inside and immediately fished out the keys.

"This is all my fault," she said as they hurried down the front steps.

"That's crazy. You didn't know Tom was a crook."

"I might have if I had been more concerned with checking his references and not so quick to hire him. But I was so hurt and angry with myself for the mistake I made with Cade, I let my pride influence my decision. Now look what's happened. And I'm responsible."

Belle had just unlocked her vehicle, slid behind the wheel and, by sheer force of habit, buckled her seat belt, when one of the ranch hands walked up.

"Miz McBride." He tipped his hat. "Reese."

"Hello, Tyler. Did you need something?"

Reese climbed into the passenger seat of the Suburban, flipped on the CB and began twisting the dial to find channel seven.

"Well, Tom Carrington's truck tore out of here—" Tyler jerked a thumb over his shoulder toward the main road "—about twenty minutes ago."

Belle offered a tight smile. "Thank you, Tyler, we know."

"Looks like Carrington is behind the recent rash of thefts in this area," Reese added.

Tyler's mouth fell open. "No kiddin'? Lord, have mercy."

Belle looked at Reese. "Rash? You mean we're not the only ones who have been robbed?"

"The old Freelander place was hit for a trailer and

feed, and the Rocking H lost some stock. Cade and I have been snooping around, trying to find out who was behind it, ever since he realized some of our horses were missing."

"Uh, Miz McBride—"

"Cade's suspected Carrington that long?"

Reese nodded.

"Miz McBride?"

"Yes, Tyler," she snapped. "What is it?"

"Well, it's just that Tom wasn't driving that truck."

"What?" Reese leaned over to look in Tyler's face. "How do you know it wasn't him?"

"That's what I was tryin' to tell Miz McBride. I seen him not five minutes ago loadin' his gear in Kyle Allen's beat-up old station wagon."

Reese quickly tuned the CB radio to channel seven, picked up the mike and depressed the talk button. "Cade? Cade, you there?"

"You got me, go ahead."

"You're following a decoy. Carrington is here, about to run. You copy?"

"Yeah." The sound of brakes screeching mixed with radio static grated on their ears, and Belle knew Cade was coming back. "What's the ETA on the sheriff's deputies?"

"Any minute."

"Don't let Carrington get away. Whatever it takes, stop him. You copy?"

"Yeah. We're on it. Out," Reese said, ending the

transmission. He jumped out of the Suburban and closed his door. "Belle, stay here in case Cade calls back. Tyler, come with me." And they took off toward the back lot.

Belle sat there listening to the static, hoping to hear Cade's voice. She picked up the mike and thought about saying something, but what could she say? He had told her once that her temper would get her into trouble, and he was right. Temper and pride. And it was her mistake. All of it.

She had practically given Carrington carte blanche to rob not only her, but her neighbors as well. She wondered what her grandfather would say now. As much as she missed him, at the moment she was glad he wasn't here to witness her shame.

The sound of a fast-moving truck yanked her out of her thoughts. Cade! She twisted in her seat in order to see the gate and main road. No. She turned back around. The sound was coming from the other side of the house. Then she saw an old beat-up station wagon barreling around the barn.

Carrington!

Belle strained to see Reese, but there was no one, no vehicle behind Tom.

Suddenly Cade's words rang in her ears. *Whatever it takes, stop him.* The next second she saw the station wagon rounding the house headed for the gate and escape. She had to do something! With a quick calculation of the distance between her and the road, plus the length of her vehicle, Belle made a decision. Her truck was expendable, but Cade wasn't. She started the Suburban, shoved it in reverse and stomped on the accelerator. The vehicle shot across the lawn, through a well-tended flower bed, and came to a screeching halt just far enough into the driveway that the rear would block Carrington's only exit. She punched the button on her shoulder strap at the same time she opened the door to scramble out of the vehicle.

But the harness didn't release.

She hit it again. And again, yanking on it with all her might, but nothing happened. Panic shot through her entire body.

Please, God, no, she prayed as she glanced up to see surprise, then fear on Tom Carrington's face a split second before the station wagon slammed into the left rear side of her truck. The force of the impact spun the Suburban sideways, slamming it into a section of pipe fence running the length of the driveway.

*Please, God, don't let me lose my baby* was Belle's last thought before she lost consciousness.

# 10

"ANY WORD YET?" Reese handed Cade his second round of vending machine coffee in as many hours.

"No," Cade replied, scrubbing his face with both hands. He blinked, then took the foam cup. Neither of them mentioned the fact that his hand was shaking.

"You've got to hang in there, ace. She's strong, and she's got guts. She'll make it. You'll see."

"But a head injury..."

"The Farentinos are notorious for their hard heads," Reese said, hoping to lighten his friend's depression.

Cade cut him a hard look. "McBride. She's a Mc-Bride."

"I just meant—"

Cade stopped him with a hand to his shoulder. "I know what you meant, and I appreciate it. It's just that I've never been this scared in my whole life. If it was me in there, no sweat." He took a deep breath. "But Belle...and the baby."

With the cup halfway to his lips, he stopped and looked up, his eyes filled with fear. "God, what if I lose them both?"

"Hey, don't even think like that. They're both going to be all right."

"No thanks to me."

"You're not responsible for what happened any more than Belle is responsible for Carrington's crimes."

"Aren't I? The things I said to her, Reese. I was so cruel."

"You were hurt."

"That's no excuse!" The outburst earned him a condemning glance from the nurse behind the emergency room admitting desk. "I'll never forgive myself for the things I said," he murmured in a calmer tone. "And neither will Belle."

"Yes, she will when you tell her you love her."

"I wonder if she would even believe me? Maybe she would have last night, if I had given her the engagement ring like I planned."

"What are you talking about?"

"I had planned to ask Belle to marry me all over again. Even bought her an engagement ring. She didn't have one, you know, and women like that kind of...stuff. But now..." He shook his head.

"C'mon, Cade. You've got to—"

The door to Belle's room opened, and her doctor stepped out. Frowning, he looked from one man to the other. "Which one of you is her husband?"

The expression on the doctor's face didn't look promising, and Cade's heart suddenly felt as if it were encased in concrete. "I—I..." His voice broke. "I am."

"McBride, isn't it?"

Cade nodded.

"Well, Mr. McBride, your wife is a very fortunate young woman. Ironically, the seat belt that trapped her in the truck also saved her life. There's no skull fracture. She does, however, have a nasty concussion, but believe me, it could have been much worse."

Cade's legs buckled, and for a minute he thought he was going to pass out from relief. "And—" He was almost afraid to ask. "And the baby? What about the baby, Doc?"

"So far, the pregnancy is stable. Dr. Jordan, her obstetrician, has examined her, and at this point he sees no cause for concern. I'd like to keep her overnight just for observation, but if everything continues on this course, she'll probably be able to go home tomorrow."

When Cade just stared at the doctor, unable to reply, Reese shook the man's hand. "Thanks, Doc. He's been in pretty bad shape waiting to hear."

"I can see that. Why don't you take him home—" the doctor removed the cup of coffee from Cade's hand, receiving no protest "—and put him to bed?"

"No!" Cade snapped out of his stupor. "I'm not going anywhere until I see Belle." His gaze focused on the doctor. "You hear me? I've got to see her."

"Easy, Mr. McBride. I wouldn't dream of stopping

you. Just remember that she goes in and out of consciousness, and she is in a lot of pain."

"Can't you give her something?"

"No. It might mask other symptoms that could develop. As well, medication could be harmful to the baby. Just think of it as the mother of all headaches. She may experience some dizziness and blurred vision at first, so you'll want to make sure you, or someone, is with her just in case. But that should clear up in two to three days."

"We'll take care of it," Reese assured him.

The doctor opened the door. "Go right in, Mr. McBride."

Cade steadied himself. With a quick glance at Reese, who gave him a smile and a thumbs-up sign, he went in to see Belle.

She looked so small and fragile lying there. Tubes dangled and apparatuses bleeped, all a terrifying reminder of how close he had come to losing her and their child. Moving to her bedside, he quietly pulled up a chair and sat down.

Gently he lifted her hand to his lips. "Please," he whispered against her cool skin. "If you can hear me, Lord, take care of them. Please." Still holding her hand, he brushed a lock of hair from her forehead.

At his touch, she stirred, moaning slightly. Cade jerked his hand back. Had he hurt her? He would rather cut his heart out than have her, or their child, suffer. They had to be all right, because nothing made any sense without them.

He tried to remember what his life had been like before loving her, but he couldn't. Nothing before her seemed important, not even his dream of owning his own land. Lust, he thought. For the land, and for Belle. That's how all this had started, and look where it had brought them.

Look where *he* had brought them.

He hadn't been satisfied with having his dream. Oh, no, he had to add her into the bargain. And to think he had accused Belle of manipulation. Who the hell did he think he was, slinging accusations at her?

Remembering the vile things he had said made him sick to his stomach.

Even if she opened her eyes this minute and he could tell her how much he loved her, he had no right to expect her to believe him. A man doesn't treat the woman he loves the way he treated her.

He hadn't realized how much he loved her until he drove through the gate and saw the driver's side of her Suburban caved in and her arm hanging out the window. If he lived to be a hundred, that moment, that scene, would be forever etched in his mind. For two heart-stopping moments until he could get to her, he thought she was dead.

But she was alive. The baby was alive.

He had no right to ask for more.

Ten minutes later he slipped quietly out of the room and closed the door.

Reese was nearby. "How is she?"

"I think...they're going to be okay."

"Did you talk to her? Did you tell her you love her like I suggested?"

"She wasn't awake."

"Well, don't worry, ace. You can tell her next time." Reese put a hand on Cade's shoulder. "How about heading home for some shut-eye, then you can come back in the morning."

"I'd rather stay here, but you go on."

Reese glanced over at the two extremely uncomfortable-looking sofas in the waiting room. "You take the one on the right, I'll take the left."

Three hours later Cade watched Reese nod off and thought to himself that he had never appreciated the depth of their friendship until now. More accurately, he hadn't appreciated Reese. Hell, when you came right down to it, he hadn't appreciated a whole lot in his life. Now, with the exception of Reese, it was a case of too little, too late.

He slipped back into Belle's room and sat by her bed until the sun came up. Until the nurse ran him out, in fact.

And sometime during the wee hours he made a promise to himself, to Belle. If she was willing to forgive him, he would spend the rest of his life trying to make it up to her.

All she had to do was let him explain.

Reese was trying to work the kinks out of his neck from sleeping on the too-short sofa when Cade came out of Belle's room.

"How is she?"

"Better. Her color's back, and she doesn't seem so restless."

"That's great. Let's celebrate with some of that god-awful stuff that passes for coffee around here."

By the time Reese returned with two lukewarm coffees, Cade was pacing the waiting room. "What's going on?"

"They think she's waking up. The nurse called the doctor, and he's in there now."

"Gets better and better."

Minutes ticked by, and Cade kept pacing and glancing at the door. Finally, the doctor came out.

"That's some tough lady you've got there, Mr. McBride. She's awake and doing very well. We're going to release her around noon."

Reese gave Cade a hearty slap on the back. "How about that, ace? Good news."

"Great." He managed a smile. "Wonderful." But he was still waiting. Waiting to see if she asked for him.

"Can we see her?" Reese asked.

"Sure." The doctor shook both their hands and left.

"Well, c'mon," Reese urged when Cade didn't move. "Don't just stand there."

"You...you go on."

"What?"

"I, uh, need to wash my face and tuck my shirt in—"

"Oh, I get it. Three's company."

"Something like that. I'll wait."

Reese grinned. "I'll say hello and be out of your hair in a jiffy."

BELLE KNEW CADE WAS waiting outside and that he was all right because the doctor had filled her in. His well-being was the subject of the second question she asked, right after "Is my baby okay?"

On the constant verge of tears ever since regaining consciousness, she leaned forward to stroke her tummy as she whispered, "I'm so sorry, and so grateful you're not hurt. I—I only wanted to help your daddy...I never would have..." Belle let her head fall back on the pillow. "Oh, thank you, God, for saving my baby."

After such a mishap, Belle knew she shouldn't tarnish her good fortune with cowardice, but she couldn't face Cade right now. She had turned his life upside down with her ridiculous scheme and lied to him about his own child. How many apologies would it take to make up for that? Even if he accepted her apologies, it wouldn't change the fact that she had probably lost any chance at making him believe she loved him.

She would have to face him, of course. There would have to be a final reckoning, and she knew it was not going to be pleasant. Her only hope was that regardless of how he now felt about her, they would be able to establish a workable situation where the baby was concerned. The thought of a future where Cade was always in her life, but never in her arms, was so depressing, she couldn't wrap her mind around the concept.

Yes, she would have to see him, but not now. She simply wasn't strong enough. Tomorrow, or the day after, when she could gather her courage and prepare herself for the inevitable heartache.

At that moment, Reese came in. "Hey there, gorgeous," he said. "How ya doing?"

"Better." She smiled.

"Had us worried for a minute. Think Cade even got a couple of gray hairs."

"The doctor told me that he got Carrington without any trouble."

"Thanks to you. That was some stunt you pulled."

Belle glanced away. "Believe me, if I had remembered how stubborn my seat belt has been lately, I never would have done it. The only good thing to come out of this was that Tom didn't get away."

When she looked up, there were tears in her eyes. "It was stupid. I was stupid. My baby could have..." Her voice broke along with the emotional dam she had held steady for so long. Tears streamed down her cheeks and she sobbed.

"Aw, Belle," Reese said. "Don't cry." He headed for the door. "Let me get Cade—"

"No! N-no."

"But he's been waiting—"

"I can't face him yet."

"What?"

"Not yet. I—I...not after...after everything. I can't."

"This is crazy. He's been—"

"Reese, I know you mean well, but you don't understand, and I'm not sure I can explain it to you. Please...I'm just not up to seeing Cade right now."

"If that's the way you want it, but—"

"That's the way I want it."

Reese shrugged and left the room.

Cade was so nervous he crammed his hands in his pockets to keep from fidgeting. "She doing okay?"

"Doing great."

"Did you tell her I was here?"

"Yeah."

"And?" Cade held his breath and prayed.

"Sorry, ace. She doesn't want to see you."

BELLE DIDN'T KNOW WHAT she had expected, but arriving at the ranch and finding Cade gone hadn't even entered her mind. She'd thought he'd wait a day or two, then come back and try to work out their differences. But not just...leave. No call. No note. Nothing.

She hadn't been able to bring herself to talk to him at the hospital. She had to be strong to face him, and at that moment, hadn't been. Now it seemed she wouldn't have to worry about facing him. So, how did she apologize to a man who had disappeared?

He had talked to Reese before he left, but his message hadn't held any comfort, much less hope. He told Reese he would be in touch, and to make sure she knew he would do right by the baby.

Do right by the baby. Not a word for her.

It certainly sounded as if he didn't intend to come back.

Which meant she might never get the chance to tell him that she loved him. Two weeks had passed with no word from Cade when Reese walked into her office packing an attitude. He didn't wait for her secretary to buzz, he just came right on in.

"All right, I've had it. I figured in three, maybe four days you and Cade would come to your senses, but obviously I was wrong. How long are you going to mope around here before you try to find him?"

"Stay out of this, Reese."

"Oh, yeah. Like I haven't been in the middle since this thing started."

"I appreciate your concern—"

"Concern? Try fatigue. Do you realize I've done most of the work since you got out of the hospital? And if you don't mind my saying so, I'm getting a little sick and tired of it. Now, I was willing to shoulder the load when you first got home, but let's face it, Belle. You've got roses in your cheeks, and you're getting fat as a pig."

She shot out of her chair. "I am not. I've hardly gained more than..."

The grin on his face could only be described as blatantly self-satisfied.

"That was mean."

"At least I got you out of that chair for some reason other than ten trips a day to the bathroom."

"That—" she couldn't help but return his smile "—is just plain bad manners."

"So—" he folded his arms across his chest "—what are you going to do about Cade?"

"What can I do? He's vanished."

"He's hiding."

"What's the difference? I can't find him. Are you sure you don't know where he is?"

"Listen, if I knew, I'd be there so fast it would make your head spin. I never know when he's going to call. He talks for five or ten minutes and refuses to tell me where he's calling from. The man is so hardheaded he could give lessons to a mule. This winery takes both of us to run it. We need him to run the ranch. Believe me, I want him back here just as bad as you do."

Glancing down, Belle patted her slightly rounded tummy. "I wouldn't bet on it."

"You do want him back, don't you?"

"Of course I do."

"And you are crazy in love with him, aren't you?"

"Of course I am, but it won't do me any good, because he doesn't love me."

Reese sighed and propped his hands on his hips. "Then tell me, if the man wasn't in love with you, why would he buy you an engagement ring?"

"I don't understand."

"The night before all hell broke loose around here, Cade intended to ask you to renew your vows. For real. He even had an engagement ring in his pocket."

"He told you this?"

"While we were waiting in the emergency room for word that you were going to be okay. I've never seen him like that, Belle. If anything had happened to you and the baby, I don't know what he would have done."

"He actually said that he...loved me?"

"Oh, yeah."

Cade loved her. Cade loved her! Three little words, and her whole world had changed. Unconsciously, she stroked her tummy. "Why didn't he tell me himself?"

"He waited for you to ask for him, and—"

"And I didn't want to see him because I was too much of a coward."

"Y'all are a pair, all right. Couple of brick walls waiting for the other to tumble."

Belle sat back down in her chair, and the tears she had been denying for days trickled down her cheeks. "I've been such a fool, Reese."

"Hey, now. Don't do that. I've got an idea that might bring him home."

She sniffed, feeling a tiny glimmer of hope. "What?"

"If you want to prove how much you love him, I think you'll have to show him."

"Fine."

"We may have to make him mad to get his attention."

Belle smiled, feeling better than she had in weeks. "What else is new?"

Reese's idea was brilliant with one minor flaw. They had to find Cade to make it work. She did take some comfort from his occasional and brief contacts, letting them know he was working and healthy. Otherwise, he could have been on the other side of the planet for all she knew.

Belle rarely shopped in Sweetwater Springs, choosing to do most of her business in Lubbock simply because there was a better variety. Especially now, since she had started buying things for the baby. But she happened to be in town one hot afternoon after transacting some business at the bank, and decided to stop at the café for a tall glass of Rubydell's lemonade.

"Won't even ask if it's hot enough for ya," the waitress said as Belle climbed onto a stool at the counter. "You look plumb wilted, sugar."

"I'm getting there. How about some lemonade?"

Rubydell smiled. "Comin' right up."

Belle picked up a menu and was fanning herself when Alvin, Smitty and Old Walt wandered in.

"Hey there, Belle. How ya doin'?"

"Fine thanks, Alvin. Afternoon, boys."

The other two offered their greetings.

Smitty sidled up to the stool next to Belle's. "Say, heard you were gonna be a mama."

"Smitty," Rubydell warned.

"It's all right. I think the whole town knows by now." She turned to the man with the toothless grin. "That's right, Smitty. I'm going to have a baby."

Alvin and Old Walt weren't ones to take a back seat

to their pal. "Well, now, ain't that fine," Alvin said. "We're mighty happy for you."

"Mighty happy. And that's a fact."

"When's it gonna come?"

"In about seven months."

Smitty slapped his knee. "Hot damn. Bet Cade's about to bust his buttons. Just wait till I see him, I'm gonna rib him good 'bout poopy diapers and 3:00 a.m. bottles."

"Well, the next time you see him, tell him I'd like to talk to him, too," Belle said.

"Sure thing."

Something in the way Smitty said that made her turn and ask, "When *did* you see Cade last?"

"Oh, three, no, four days ago."

Alvin and Old Walt's ears pricked up. Alvin narrowed his eyes. "You're foolin'."

"No, I ain't."

"Never mentioned it before now."

"Don't tell you everythin'."

"Smitty," Belle interrupted. "This is important. Where did you see Cade?"

"New Deal. Go up there every week to visit my daughter and those teenage brats of hers."

"New Deal. You're sure?"

"Yep. He's working at the feed store."

Belle leaned over and kissed Smitty on the cheek, then left the café in a hurry.

"Well, don't that beat all," the old man said, touching his cheek.

THREE DAYS LATER, Belle was beginning to doubt Cade would take the bait Joseph Worthington had delivered. She couldn't believe he had been fewer than fifty miles away the entire time.

Fifty miles!

In less than an hour she could have been in his arms, telling him how much she loved him. Her frustration level practically shot through the roof. She was torn between wanting to strangle him, or smother him with kisses. Of course, she was betting on the latter, but knowing Cade's stubborn streak, she might have to strangle him to get his attention.

Then, on the fourth day, almost at dusk, Belle glanced out the bay window of her grandfather's study and saw a vehicle coming down the main road. Coming fast.

Her heart rate jumped, and she swallowed hard. Cade's truck shot through the gate, raced up the driveway and came to a screeching halt. He got out of the truck and slammed the door.

Oh, my, Belle thought, steeling herself for his entrance.

He didn't even knock, but came through the front door very much the same way he had the last time.

"Belle!"

She waited, knowing he would find her.

"I know you're here," he roared. "Dammit, Belle, answer me."

As she sat behind the big mahogany desk, her hands were shaking so badly she clasped them together in her lap, and she pursed her lips together to keep from shouting "I'm in here." She could hear him stomping through the foyer, probably headed for the kitchen, but then he stopped. And started coming her way.

Breathe deeply, she told herself.

He came through the door and covered the distance to the desk in three long strides. She half expected to see him breathing fire. He slammed a legal-sized envelope down on the desk so hard the ashtray rattled.

"What the hell do you think you're doing?"

"Hello, Cade. It's good to see you."

He blinked but wouldn't be sidetracked. "Answer me." He pointed to the envelope. "What the hell is this?"

"Business. A matter that needed to be settled. A loose end that needed attention, you might say."

"Loose end? Have you gone insane?"

"That's not very nice, Cade. And no, I don't think so."

"Nice!" Why was she smiling? "You really are insane."

"I just answered that question. Was there something else I can do for you?"

He stared at her for a second, trying to decide if she really was insane. Then he picked up the envelope. "I'm not signing these." Then he tore it in half and flung both halves back on the desktop.

"There. Now everything is back to normal. You've

got the winery, and that's the way it's supposed to be.
If you're trying to force me out of your life, you win.
But you're *not* divorcing me, do you hear? This is
your dream, and you're going to have it. You are not
giving up anything, and that's final!"

She stood up.

Cade's gaze automatically went to her stomach,
and he went white as a sheet.

Perfect. Just the effect she was hoping for. The
denim maternity jumper and bandanna-print T-shirt
couldn't be mistaken for anything other than what it
was. She pushed back her chair, walked around the
desk, then across the room to stand beside the tasting
chair.

"I have no intention of giving up anything. Not the
winery, not the baby. Not you." She started toward
him, wearing the same kind of cocky grin that looked
so good on him.

"Belle? What are you doing?"

"Prepare yourself, cowboy. You're about to be offered the deal of a lifetime."

"I don't know what's going on here, but—Belle?
Don't smile at me like that. And I can't say I like that
look in your eyes, either."

She kept smiling. "Yes, you do."

"Stop telling me what I like and what I don't like."

"Somebody's got to."

"Not you. I didn't come here today to—"

"Why did you come?"

"You know damned good and well why I came.

I'm not going to allow you to hand the winery over to your uncle and his sons, just because—"

"Because what?"

"Because you think you owe me something. So, take whatever deal you've hatched in that devious little mind of yours and make someone else's life miserable."

Devious, huh? He didn't know the half of it. "Are you miserable, Cade?"

He took another step back. "Damn straight."

As he had once done to her, she backed him up against the edge of the desk. They were practically toe-to-toe. "Well, to quote you, 'Get used to it,' because I haven't even gotten started yet."

"Belle, please. Don't do this." Despite his good intentions not to touch her, he couldn't resist slipping his arms around her. "I don't want us to hurt each other anymore. Think of the baby."

"Oh, I am. And you were right when you said I was insane." She rose up on tiptoe and put her arms around his neck. "I am completely, totally, hopelessly insane about you. And if you would stop trying to save me from myself for three seconds, you could tell me how crazy you are about me."

Cade stared at her, his mind scrambling to make sense out of her words. "Did...did you just say you were...crazy about me?"

"It's worse than that. I love you."

"Y-you—"

"Love you. With all my heart and soul."

Cade looked into her eyes and felt his heart swell. A second later his mouth took hers in a sweet re-union. "I love you, Belle. Nothing is any good without you. I'm no good without you."

"And I'm lost without you."

And so this was it, she thought, gazing into his eyes. This was what she had fought against, and longed for at the same time. No more abandonment. He was hers forever.

First she had set the rules, then he had changed them. From now on, she realized they would have to make them up as they went along, because there simply weren't any rules for what they had. From the beginning, they hadn't fit the mold, and she doubted they ever would. But that was all right. She had discovered life was dull without a little wildness now and then.

"We'll have to work hard to keep our pride from getting in the way."

He cupped her face in his hands. "I know, but I wouldn't want you without it."

"Same here. And I'm sure we'll argue."

"Yeah, but making up is the best part."

As Cade kissed her deeply, thoroughly, his hands slid down her back and around to her tummy. Everything he wanted in the world was right here in his hands.

He drew back and looked into her eyes, then abruptly set her from him.

"Cade?"

Before she realized what he was doing, he was down on one knee.

"What are you doing?"

"What does it look like I'm doing? We've been doing everything backward from the beginning. I'm not taking any more chances."

He took her hand. "Isabella Farentino McBride, will you marry me?"

She grabbed a handful of his shirt and brought him back up where he belonged. In her arms. "Yes."

When he started to kiss her again, she put her hand on his chest. "Just promise me one thing."

"What's that?"

"That we won't go camping for our next honeymoon."

"You got a deal, so long as we lock up all the guns."

Three weeks later, as the sun was setting over the caprock, guests sat under a decorated awning waiting to see Mr. and Mrs. Cade McBride become Mr. and Mrs. Cade McBride.

Inside, dressed in the same clothes he had worn for his first wedding, Cade paced the foyer, checking his watch every two minutes. Reese looked on with bemused pity.

Cade stopped pacing. "You've got the ring, right?"

Reese held up his right pinkie finger, displaying a plain gold band and two diamond ring guards. "Will you settle down? You're making me nervous."

"And Posey promised to let you know when Belle was set to come downstairs, right?"

"Yes, but you're not supposed to see the bride before the wedding."

"We're already married, what difference does it make? Besides—" he adjusted his bolo tie with the onyx stone set in silver for the fourth time "—I have to give her something before the ceremony."

"Let me have whatever it is, and I'll make sure she gets it."

Cade shook his head. "No. *I* have to give it to her."

"You know, I pity your poor child. The kid doesn't stand a chance with two hardheaded parents. Say, that's not a bad name for the kid. Chance. Think I'll mention it to Belle." At Cade's glare, he threw up his hands. "Just a suggestion from a self-appointed uncle. But I can see my talents are not appreciated. Do it like you want to."

"Exactly."

At that moment, Posey motioned from the top of the stairs.

"Get lost, Reese."

"Fine thing to say to your best man." But he left smiling.

"Cade."

At the sound of Belle's voice, he turned and almost forgot to breathe. She was absolutely stunning. He still couldn't believe his good luck. By some twist of fate, he had found the kind of love he had once thought was for fools.

"Don't move," he said, coming up to meet her.

"How do I look?" Since she couldn't fit into her first wedding dress, her seamstress had taken the lace from that gown and incorporated it into the high-waisted second dress. "Not too fat?"

"Gorgeous."

"I'm going to remind you of that when I'm so big I can't see my toes and you have to help me out of a chair."

"I can't wait." He took her arm and guided her down the stairs.

Belle took a deep breath. "Are you nervous?"

"Are you?"

"A little."

"Me, too," he admitted. "This is our real wedding. The other was—"

"Don't even think about using the word *mistake*, Cade McBride."

"Darlin', if that was a mistake, I hope our life is filled with them. No, I was going to say the first one was great, but this one has more meaning. I love you, Belle. And I promise to spend the rest of my life loving you, and doing my best to make you happy. That doesn't mean I'll always succeed, but..."

He turned around, opened a box and lifted out a very special surprise gift. Two bouquets of sweetheart roses and baby's breath had been joined together to make one. Gently he placed it in her hands. "I'm learning."

With tears in her eyes she leaned forward and kissed him softly. "I love you."

An hour later the happy couple wandered among their friends and neighbors, who had gathered to wish them well.

"Some shindig." Alvin Dellworthy craned his head to scan the crowd.

Old Walt nodded. "Ain't seen this many folks in one place since the county fair."

"See all that food and wine they got laid out?" Smitty smacked his lips. "We're gonna feast tonight, boys."

Belle and Cade strolled up to where the three men stood.

Smitty grinned and tipped his hat. "Mighty nice weddin'."

Cade squeezed his wife's hand. "We thought so."

"I reckon you two will have your hands full, what with Belle runnin' the winery and you back bein' foreman."

"I won't be running the winery full-time," she told Alvin. "Of course, Reese is my right arm. But my college roommate is also moving here from Austin to help me out until the baby comes. She's practically a genius when it comes to business of any kind." Belle looked up into the face of her husband. "And who knows, I might decide motherhood is every bit as fulfilling as making wine and have to try it again."

Cade smiled. "You can do anything you put your mind to."